INVESTIGATE AWAY

JAGAR'S STORY

THE EMERALD CITY SERIES

JEN TALTY

JUPITER PRESS

This book is a work of fiction. Names, characters, places, and incidents are products of the author's imagination or used fictitiously. Any resemblance to actual events or locales or persons living or dead is entirely coincidental.

Copyright © 2020 by Jen Talty All rights reserved.

No part of this work may be used, stored, reproduced or transmitted without written permission from the publisher except for brief quotations for review purposes as permitted by law. This book is licensed for your personal enjoyment only. This book may not be re-sold or given away to other people. If you would like to share this book with another person, please purchase an additional copy for each recipient. If you're reading this book and did not purchase it, or it was not purchased for your use only, please purchase your own copy.

Publishing History: Originally published by Lady Boss Press.

INVESTIGATE AWAY
THE EMERALD CITY SERIES

Jagar's Story
Book 1

USA Today Bestselling Author
JEN TALTY

PRAISE FOR JEN TALTY

"Deadly Secrets is the best of romance and suspense in one hot read!" *NYT Bestselling Author Jennifer Probst*

"A charming setting and a steamy couple heat up the pages in a suspenseful story I couldn't put down!" *NY Times and USA today Bestselling Author Donna Grant*

"Jen Talty's books will grab your attention and pull you into a world of relatable characters, strong personalities, humor, and believable storylines. You'll laugh, you'll cry, and you'll rush to get the next book she releases!" Natalie Ann USA Today Bestselling Author

"I positively loved *In Two Weeks*, and highly recommend it. The writing is wonderful, the story is fantastic, and the characters will keep you coming back for more. I can't wait to get my hands on future installments of the NYS Troopers series." *Long and Short Reviews*

"*In Two Weeks* hooks the reader from page one. This is a fast paced story where the development of the romance grabs you emotionally and the suspense keeps you sitting on the edge of your chair. Great characters, great writing, and a believable plot that can be a warning to all of us." *Desiree Holt, USA Today Bestseller*

"*Dark Water* delivers an engaging portrait of wounded hearts as the memorable characters take you on a healing journey of love. A mysterious death brings danger and intrigue into the drama, while sultry passions brew into a believable plot that melts the reader's heart. Jen Talty pens an entertaining romance that grips the heart as the colorful and dangerous story unfolds into a chilling ending." *Night Owl Reviews*

"This is not the typical love story, nor is it the typical mystery. The characters are well rounded and interesting." *You Gotta Read Reviews*

"Murder in Paradise Bay is a fast-paced romantic thriller with plenty of twists and turns to keep you guessing until the end. You won't want to miss this one..." *USA Today bestselling author Janice Maynard*

NOTE FROM JEN TALTY

Investigate Away was originally published as *Investigate With Me* in the Kristen Proby With Me Universe in 2020. I have rewritten the story, removing any and all elements and characters from Kristen's universe, and added some bonus material.

BOOK DESCRIPTION

Not much happens in the city of Langley, especially in the dead of winter, and that's precisely the way newly assigned Chief of Police Jagar Bowie prefers it.

For years, Jag served the city of Seattle as one of its finest homicide detectives. He solved more murders than anyone else in his department. But it was the one he hadn't solved that ruined his career and still haunted his dreams. No matter how hard he tries, he can't stop searching for the Trinket Killer.

And he can't get Callie Dixon out of his heart.

When Callie Dixon returned to Seattle to finish her

book about her time as a reporter covering the Trinket Killer, her own sister's death, and the police officer who botched the case and stole her heart, she never expected history would repeat itself.

But that's exactly what happened.

And now her life, and heart are on the line.

For Chelle Olson. You always manage to make me smile, laugh, and you always give me strength when I need it most. Your friendship is gold.

PROLOGUE

Callie Dixon took a step back, planted her hands on her hips, and stared at the pictures of eleven different women she'd tacked up on a corkboard in her one-bedroom apartment. All of them were between twenty-five and thirty years of age. All blond. All slender in build and pretty. Two of the women were lawyers. Two worked as top executives for tech companies. One was in medical school. One a forensic lab specialist for the police department. Two more were professors at a local college, and the latest victim owned a series of upscale salons in downtown.

"Babe, I caught the bastard. What the hell are you doing?"

Callie sat on the edge of her bed and glanced

over her shoulder. If anyone had told her that she'd end up in bed with Detective Jagar Bowie, she would have laughed in their face. Jag had to be the most arrogant, self-absorbed police officer she'd ever interviewed.

For the few years during the Trinket Killer investigations, she and Jag had not always played nice in the sandbox. As a matter of fact, they had tossed a few choice words at each other—more than once. He hated the way she'd covered the murders in the media, mostly because he thought it made both him and the police department look bad.

But at the end of the day, he was a damn good detective.

Jag was an incredibly sexy man with his thick dark hair, almond-shaped chocolate eyes, and five-o'clock shadow that he couldn't shave away even if he took a razor to his face three times a day.

"It doesn't feel right. It's too neat. Don't you think?"

"Oh, for fuck's sake. What are you talking about?"

If she told him what she was *really* thinking, he'd be pissed as hell, and then he'd get dressed and leave, never to return again. But if she said nothing, she felt as if she was doing all of these dead girls a disservice. Her job as an investigative reporter was to not only report the news, but also to help aid in the resolution of crime. "I don't think you caught the right man. I mean, I'm sure Adam Wanton did something criminal, but I feel like this is all some sort of setup."

"Are we really going to start this bullshit again? We have so much evidence, both forensic and DNA. I know I can sleep easy tonight." He punched one of the pillows and moved to a sitting position. "The case is closed. The Trinket Killer is behind bars. I've got my man. You broke the story first. Now, will you come back to bed?"

She scooted to the headboard, but she couldn't let it go. Jag might have arrested someone, and she knew he was good at his job.

But something prickled the back of her mind.

Unfortunately, she'd seen much of the evidence that Jag had mentioned, and she had to agree that, on the surface, it all pointed to Adam.

Jag wrapped his thick arms around her body and kissed her shoulder. "Please, babe. Take the pictures down. You'll feel better, trust me."

"Be honest with me, Jag. Do you really think this is wrapped up with the perfect bow?"

"Wanton admitted it. He knew things." Jag let out a long breath. "What's still bothering you?"

"The lack of trinkets. Where are they?"

"What?" Jag smacked his forehead. "He leaves them with the body; he doesn't collect them. Why are we still having this conversation?"

"Don't you think it's odd that a killer who leaves dolphin trinkets behind, who bought out an entire store, doesn't have any in his home or car or office?"

"Maybe a little. But DNA doesn't lie," Jag said.

Callie couldn't argue that point.

Detective Jagar Bowie of the Seattle Police Department followed the young officer through the woods. A faint layer of thin fog floated in the beams of flashlights. He glanced at the sky. The moon and the stars danced behind a layer of clouds, trying to shine their light on the scene below.

"A group of teenagers found the body when they were looking for a place to party," the officer said. "They freaked out and ran to the parking lot where they called 9-1-1."

"Where are they now?" Jag asked.

The officer pointed to a clearing about a quarter mile from the sound in Seward Park. Ajax Bond huddled with another detective and one of the CSI techs. He gave a slight nod.

"We moved them away from the media. How the hell did Callie and her camera crew get here so fast?" the officer asked.

"She's a shark." Jag couldn't say it was because she was sleeping in his bed. Besides, that was only part of the reason. Ever since Adam Wanton had been released on a technicality two days ago, she was on the warpath.

At least she'd finally come around to the idea that he was the killer since the murders had stopped once Adam had been locked up.

But now that he was out, Callie was just sitting around and waiting for Adam to strike again so she could rip the police a new asshole for how they'd botched the DNA evidence. He nearly choked on his thoughts. DNA didn't lie, but when you didn't follow protocol, the proof got tossed, and then you had no fucking case, and a killer got to walk free.

He wasn't the one who'd bungled the evidence, but it *was* his case. He had screwed up the arrest, and the buck stopped with him.

"She doesn't like cops," the officer said as Ajax made his way toward Jag.

He'd thought that about her as well until he got to know her better. "That's really not true. She just gets frustrated with the system. And right now, I can't blame her." Of course, when they first started sleeping together, it had been just that.

Sex.

And really good sex.

But slowly it developed into something he'd never experienced before. They decided to keep their relationship to themselves, simply because it was so new to both of them.

"You're defending Callie?" Ajax stepped in front of him and stretched out his hand. "Since when? You can't stand that snake."

Jag turned. Callie's news van was parked as close as the barricade would allow. He could barely see her silhouette through the trees. Once you got past her tough exterior, there was a really wonderful woman underneath. She had a big heart; she just kept it guarded. He could understand that. "Right now, I'm pretty annoyed with how our system works, especially because I assume you're going to tell me that our victim is blond, a professional, and is holding a cheap dolphin trinket in her right hand."

"You're right. I am." Ajax was new to homicide but not to being a detective.

"Fuck," Jag mumbled.

"She's over here." Ajax pointed to where the medical examiner and his team had laid out a body bag and gurney.

"Any identifying marks? Or anything we can use to find out who she is?"

"We're running her prints. But she has a tattoo on her wrist. It's an infinity shape with the words *sisters forever* weaved into it."

Oh fuck. How many women had tattoos like that? He suspected not many. Jag sucked in a deep breath and let it out slowly. He did it five times, each time clearing his mind a little more. Seeing a dead body never got any easier. It never got different.

And he never became numb to it.

Seeing a friend murdered sent him down a road he'd never navigated.

He swallowed as Callie came into view, her face turned the other way.

Careful not to disturb any potential evidence, Jag

circled the body, slowing as he approached the head. Her thick blond hair partially obscured her face. He knelt down and gasped. "No, no, no," he whispered, shaking his head. "Shit." He stood. "Damn it."

"What is it?" Ajax asked.

"I know her." Tears stung the back of his eyes. He pushed air out of his lungs and tried to take a deep breath. "Her name is Stephanie Dixon. She's Callie's—the reporter from Channel 5—sister."

"Motherfucker," Ajax said. "I didn't know she had a sister. How do you know she has a sister?"

"Long story." Jag leaned against a tree. "Does anyone have eyes on Adam?"

Ajax shook his head. "Do you think Adam knew Callie had a sister and targeted her?"

"I don't know, but that puts Callie in his crosshairs. Not to mention, she meets his criteria." Jag rubbed the side of his face. "Before this gets out of hand, I should go get Callie."

"I don't think that's a good idea."

"She'll never forgive me if I don't." Jag pushed himself from the tree.

"Why would you care? She hates you."

Jag chuckled. "You know how you've been busting my balls about having a secret girlfriend for the last two months?"

"Yeah. So?"

"Well, not only did I go and get a girlfriend, I got myself engaged a few hours ago." He paused for emphasis. "To Callie."

"No fucking way. You and Callie?" Ajax asked with wide eyes. "How did that happen?"

"No idea. But I'm in love with her, and I can't let her stand up there and report on a dead body when she doesn't know it's her sister." Jag had delivered more bad news than a Navy chaplain. Another thing that never got easier.

But he suspected this would be about the worst thing he'd ever had to do in his life.

A large crowd had gathered in the parking lot. Many whispered and tossed about the words *Trinket Killer.* He wasn't surprised that everyone had already jumped to that conclusion.

As soon as Callie saw him, she waved to her cameraman, who immediately flipped on his light.

Jag gave her the cut sign. "I need to talk to you. Alone."

She handed her mic to someone and timidly made her way toward him. "What's going on? You shouldn't be pulling me aside like this. People will start talking."

"Let them. I don't care." He curled his fingers

around her biceps and tugged her down the path until he knew they were out of sight of the rest of the crew, who would be doing their best to figure out why a cop would pick one reporter to bring over to the other side of the crime scene tape. He paused and held Callie steady. He stared deep into her eyes. "I love you."

"You pulled me aside to tell me that?" She turned.

"Callie. I need to tell you something about the victim." He grabbed her by the forearms. "Babe, this isn't good."

"What isn't good?" She blinked. "I appreciate all that you do, but don't go out of your way to get me an exclusive."

"Oh, sweetheart." He pulled her close. "I'm so sorry, babe. I don't know how to tell you this."

"Tell me what? Just spit it out, before my crew comes looking for me, thinking you kidnapped me or something."

He cupped her face. "It's your sister. It's Stephanie."

"What about my sister?"

"She's the victim."

"What kind of cruel joke are you playing?" She shoved his hands to the side.

This was harder than anything he's ever had to do in his career.

In his life.

"Callie, babe." He held her wrist, tracing her matching tattoo. "I know it's Stephanie because of this."

Her fist came down on his chest. "What? No. It can't be. We just had breakfast with her this morning. She was giving you shit for… for…" Callie took a step back. "You've made a mistake. It's not Stephanie."

Jag looped his arm around Callie and led her toward the body. The medical examiner and his team respectfully took a step back.

Ajax, however, stayed in his place, inching a little closer to Jag.

"Oh, my God. Stephanie," Callie cried, starting to drop to her knees a little too close to the body.

"It's still a crime scene." Jag caught her and pulled her back a little. "I'm so sorry, Callie."

She turned into his body and buried her face in his chest. "Adam Wanton did this."

"I'm afraid not," Ajax said.

"What?" Jag said. "That's impossible."

"The body that was found yesterday morning mutilated in that back alley downtown? Turns out, that was Adam. If you all had breakfast with Stephanie this morning, there is no way Adam could have killed your sister."

"I knew he wasn't the Trinket Killer, but you didn't want to listen to me. *You* always brushed my thoughts under the rug, yet I was right all along, wasn't I." Callie glanced up at Jag, tucking her long blond hair behind an ear. Her expression turned hard and cold. She pursed her lips. "You did this," she said, venom dripping from every word. She poked him in the chest. "Because of your arrogance. Because of your bad police work. Because of you, my sister is dead. I'm going to make sure you pay for this, Jagar Bowie, if it's the last thing I do."

1

A YEAR LATER...

Jagar Bowie leaned against the bar and sipped his scotch on the rocks, letting the dark liquid burn the back of his throat before swallowing. He stared across the banquet hall. Ajax Bond hadn't wanted a big send-off, but he'd been a staple in the Seattle Police Department for as long as Jag could remember, and when you're married to one of the world's most popular singers on the globe, people came out in droves when you had a party. Lorre was kind of a big deal.

Ajax had just become a detective when Jag hit the streets as a beat cop. Shortly after, Jag followed Ajax, and they worked together in the property crimes division before Jag decided that homicide was more his thing. Oddly enough, Ajax gave homicide a good college try, but when the lovebug hit him, Ajax turned in his badge to be with Lorre.

Jag couldn't blame him, but he sure as shit missed the hell out of him.

"You look like you're sulking," Ajax said as he slapped him on the back, waving to the bartender. "Another round of whatever this asshole is drinking."

"Sure thing, Mr. Bond," the bartender said.

Jag raised his glass. "Why the hell did you have to go and invite her?" He downed the last of his drink, taking in a hunk of ice with the last gulp.

"I didn't," Ajax said with a frown.

"She sent me a draft of her book this week. She wants to interview me all official-like for it."

"Jesus. Are you going to? I mean, I heard the title was going to be something like: *The Trinket Killer, Seattle's Finest's Only Unsolved Case.*"

"That's what it says on the first page." Jag had read the introduction, which had been written by some forensic specialist with the FBI. It was informative, and Jag couldn't argue with the content—or the statistics.

But he resented the hell out of the last paragraph.

Through a series of unfortunate mistakes regarding the collection and storage of DNA samples by the Seattle Police Department and the subsequent mishandling of the arrest and release of Adam Wanton—a person of interest in the case— the Trinket Killer is still at large. The lead detective on the case, Jagar Bowie, had an impeccable record. This is his only unsolved case.

"Are you going to read it?" Ajax asked.

"Probably." For months, Jag had been tortured by the lingering memories of the night they'd found Stephanie's body. His entire world had flipped upside down in a heartbeat. "The Trinket Killer is still out there."

"Don't you think it's odd that he hasn't killed in a year?"

Jag shook his head. "We don't know that he hasn't. He could be anywhere in the world." Jag had done extensive searches, looking for similar crimes, but he'd come up empty-handed every time. "He's out there, somewhere, lurking in the shadows, waiting to strike." Hindsight was twenty-twenty, and Jag should have seen it, but Callie had been right about him and his arrogance and how it affected his ability to see the problems with the case. She'd been right to question him, but his ego wouldn't listen back then. He had the best arrest record in the department, and he wanted to keep it that way.

"The Trinket Killer isn't your problem anymore," Ajax said.

Jag arched a brow. "No, it's my nightmare." He tipped back his drink and said a small prayer to the man upstairs that Callie wasn't headed in his direction.

But, as usual, no one was listening.

"You want me to stick around and play referee?" Ajax asked.

"Nope." Jag slammed his glass on the bar. "Next time you and Lorre are in town, come out to Whidbey Island. It's really peaceful out there."

"Will do."

Jag gave Ajax his best one-armed bro hug before he made a beeline for the door. No way in hell was he going to let Callie corner him. The last time he'd seen her had been at her sister's funeral, and Callie had made it very clear that she wanted nothing to do with him. She'd actually said if she never laid eyes on him again, it would be too soon.

Not to mention, she'd gone off the rails during a live broadcast, tearing into him and how he'd handled the case, exposing their relationship, and making his actions look more than questionable. He was lucky he was able to get the job on Whidbey.

The salty, cool evening air of Seattle filled his nostrils as he jogged down the steps toward the parking lot where his motorcycle awaited. He'd catch the early ferry, which would get him to his house by the time the ten o'clock news started.

Perfect timing.

"Jag," a familiar female voice rang out.

Fuck. He could keep walking and ignore her, but then the whole way home, he'd hear his mother's voice in his head as his conscience reminded him that a Bowie didn't run from their problems and they were always respectful.

He spun on his heel. "Hey, Callie," he said.

"Surprised to see me?"

He nodded. "More surprised that you're chasing me down."

"I hear congratulations are in order, Chief."

He shrugged. "It was time for a change of pace. Langley is a nice, quiet town, and I love being away from the city." Not wanting to stand idle, he continued toward his bike. "What brings you back to Seattle? Last I heard, you'd moved to San Francisco with Kara. She was a real hottie."

"We did, but I'm here for a month to finish my

book." Callie let out a sarcastic laugh. "You know she bats for the other team, so keep your dick in your pants."

"My dick is no longer your concern."

"Thank God for small favors," she said. "Did you get my book?"

He nodded.

"Have you read it?"

"No. And I don't plan to read a smear campaign either. I mean Jesus, Callie, the title alone is a dig at my career." He snagged his helmet and tucked it under his arm. "I don't understand why you thought I'd be interested in reading your twisted view on how I botched the case when we both know I did everything by the book, with the exception of two things." He held up his index finger. "And one of them I had no control over. But because I was lead, I took sole responsibility. But that's not why the case is unsolved, and you know it."

"You rushed the arrest, which is what started the ball rolling on a potential mistrial. And we both now know that it was all a setup with the DNA being contaminated from the beginning by the—"

He held up his hand. "I don't need you to tell me for the hundredth time how and where I fucked up. Trust me, I know. I have to live with the knowledge that the murderer's still out there every day. Now, if you'll excuse me, I have a ferry to catch."

Her long, warm fingers curled around his biceps.

He glanced down and looked at her short nails painted a light pink. "Let go, please."

"I didn't beat you up that bad."

"Operative words being *that bad*," he said as he let out an exasperated sigh. "What exactly do you want?"

"I want you to read the book, tell me what you think, maybe give me a quote."

He laughed. "That, my love," he said with a heavy dose of sarcasm. "Is never going to happen."

"Then how about helping me find my sister's killer, because I've dug up some things, and I'm not sure what to do with the information."

"Sorry, I'm no longer in homicide. My last girlfriend helped get me fired."

She laughed, shaking her head. "You were never fired, though perhaps I went a little too far with some of the things I said on the air. I'm sorry for that."

"That apology is a little too late." He tossed his leg over his bike and flipped up the kickstand. He hated to admit how much he'd missed Callie's sweet face and her plump lips pressed against his in a passionate kiss. The engagement ring he'd bought for her still burned a hole in his underwear drawer. He knew he should probably sell it or something, but he just couldn't get rid of it.

Not yet.

"If it makes you feel any better, I don't think any news show would have me as a reporter," she said.

"But you got a book deal, which will lead to more, which will eventually get you back in front of the camera." He twisted the key and flipped the switch before pressing the on button.

The engine purred like a kitten.

"We both know Adam Wanton wasn't the Trinket Killer and that he didn't kill my sister. But we never once considered that the Trinket Killer didn't work alone."

"Actually, I did," Jag said. "I didn't tell you everything. Just because we shared a bed, didn't mean I was going to jeopardize my case and job to give you an exclusive. I bent the rules enough as it was. However, the idea of a partner was ruled out based on DNA."

"Evidence that was planted at the crime scenes, all in an effort to make—"

"Just stop." Jag had spent the last six months going over every piece of evidence, chasing down every possible lead on his free time, then following up on things he used to think were ridiculous. If anyone thought he'd been consumed by the Trinket Killer case before, they'd lock him up and toss away the key now. "You and I have been down this road before, and it never ends well."

A day didn't go by where he didn't turn over any tiny pebble he could in search of Stephanie's killer. He'd find her murderer eventually, and he'd put him in his grave.

And then he'd turn in his badge and fly somewhere tropical, where he'd live out his days drinking fruity alcoholic beverages with umbrellas.

"Please. Read the book and then call me. I put my new cell number and a note at the end of the book," she said.

He pinched the bridge of his nose. "Why is it so important to you that I read that damn fucking garbage?"

"Because I need your help finding my sister's killer."

Callie tossed her purse into the back of her Jeep. The sound of Jag's motorcycle echoed in the night. She missed him almost as much as she missed her sister. For months before the Trinket Killer case took center stage, she and Jag had gone tit for tat. He didn't like the way she reported the news.

And she didn't like his arrogance.

But one night, when he was off duty and she wasn't covering a story, they'd found themselves in the same bar, each sipping a scotch on the rocks, in a heated discussion about police procedure and reporters and how they aren't a good mix. Next thing she knew, she was ripping off her shirt and tossing it recklessly to the floor of his apartment.

Their relationship was up and down to say the least. It wasn't until the Trinket Killer that they really started working on the same side, only she didn't know then that he was keeping things from her.

And he didn't know she was doing the same.

It had all come to a head when her sister was murdered.

"I told you going to him wouldn't be useful," Kara said, slipping into the passenger seat. "I didn't think we should come back here at all. He's let this go. I've let this go. *You* should let this go."

"If that were totally true for you, why did you bother to come back with me?" Callie asked but didn't wait for a response. "I know him, and he's still living this every day, and it's eating him like it is me." If Callie could go back in time and change how she'd responded to her sister's murder and the way she'd treated Jag, she'd do it in a heartbeat. "And let's not forget, he might have screwed up the arrest, but he didn't botch the DNA. I still think the Trinket Killer wanted us to go after Adam all along. I think the killer played us. I just need to figure out why."

"The book is all but done. I think you should take a vacation. Go to Hawaii or maybe Mexico, but you need a break. Look at what one did for me." Kara too had had her life turned upside down by the Trinket Killer. Her husband had been one of the earliest victims, and that's how Callie had met Kara and how they'd subsequently ended up working together at the station and then on her book.

Callie laughed. "Getting laid helped, huh?" She pulled the Jeep into traffic and headed toward the hotel where Kara and her boyfriend Ivan were staying.

"Hey. It's more than that." Kara reached out and squeezed Callie's thigh. "Besides, it's not just putting to rest the Trinket Killer, but you need to let Jag go. He's not worth the space in your brain. He wasn't there for you when you needed him most."

That wasn't true. From the second she'd seen her sister lying on the ground, dead, she'd made the snap decision to blame Jag. It hadn't been totally conscious, but she needed to place her anger and rage somewhere. Stephanie had called her three times the night she'd died, and all three times, Callie had ignored the call.

Why?

She'd been too busy accepting a marriage proposal.

"I don't have feelings for him anymore, but he's a good cop, and he can help me find my sister's—and your late friend's—killer." Callie rolled to a stop in the circle in front of a high-rise in the heart of downtown Seattle.

"I've been meaning to talk to you about that," Kara said as she gathered her belongings from the back seat. "Nothing we do will bring Renee back. Or Stephanie. I need to live in the present, and Ivy is real, live flesh and blood."

"What are you saying?" Callie really didn't need

Kara to spell it out. She could sense a kiss-off a mile away, but she needed Kara to say the words. They'd been through too much together.

"I'm in love with Ivy." Kara jumped from the Jeep and held up her hands. "We're talking about getting married, and she wants us to stay in San Francisco."

"That's wonderful. I'm really happy for you." That wasn't a lie. Callie truly wished the best for Kara and her new girlfriend. It would suck to continue this endeavor without her, but Callie wouldn't quit. Not until Stephanie's murderer was brought to justice.

"Are you?"

"Yes, Kara. I am." Callie smiled. "I doubt I'll ever get Jag to give me a quote or even let me interview him, so I'll be sending the final draft to the publisher soon. The reality is, our work together is done, but I'm going to miss you so much."

"What are you going to do after the book is published?" Kara asked. "And please don't say you plan on staying here."

"That's doubtful, but I will be doing a second book," Callie said. "I'll need a researcher. What can I do to interest you in that?"

Kara shook her head. "You know why I did this,

but I realized that we may never find the Trinket Killer, and I have to accept that. Getting out of Seattle this past year has been the best thing I've ever done for myself. I think my research days are over; however, I'm committed to finishing this book."

"I understand." Callie shifted the Jeep into gear. "I'll talk to you tomorrow." With tears burning the back of her eyes, Callie pulled out into city traffic and headed for the Whidbey Island Ferry. She wasn't going to let Jag off that easy. They'd both made a lot of mistakes, but she knew him, and she knew, without a doubt, that he hadn't given up on finding the Trinket Killer.

Or, at least, she had to believe that.

Because if he had, if he'd really given up on everything he'd felt for her, then she'd really done what her sister had accused her of doing. She'd officially shut out everyone who cared about her.

She pulled into the ferry line, shocked to see that Jag was in one of the first lines. Hopefully, he didn't see her in the far lane. She pulled her hair into a ponytail and tucked it under a baseball cap. Minutes later, the first lane of cars filtered onto the ferry. She watched as Jag disappeared onto the boat. It would be a good fifteen minutes before she was loaded, and she opted to stay in her car for the entire ride.

Once she was off-loaded, she made her way into the small town of Langley, where she'd booked a room at the Saratoga Inn, not far from where she'd discovered that the new chief of police had rented a house. She told herself that she'd come out here to finish the final edits on the book. That she just needed some peace and quiet.

But the reality was... she wanted—no—she needed to be close to Jag. She'd made two really big mistakes in her life.

The first had been not trusting her instincts.

The second had been walking away from him when they needed each other.

She checked herself into the inn, thankful to have a room on the top floor that overlooked the sound. She'd always loved the island off the coast of Seattle. When she and Jag had first started dating, they often took the ferry to Whidbey Island to go camping. It was a nice way for them to get away from their lives in Seattle and be a couple.

Both had agreed that it was best to keep their love affair private, at least at first, but a few months into it, she'd started to think it seemed weird.

He didn't.

They fought about it, and then as the bodies piled up during the Trinket Killer case, the secrecy became a necessity.

She tucked her cell into her back pocket and strolled down the lane toward the side street off the main road in Langley. She'd found out that Jag lived on the corner of Earl and Peach Street, which was less than a mile from the inn. She strolled through the neighborhood, sipping the wine she'd put in a Solo cup. Anything to take the edge off.

A light layer of clouds glided across the sky, dimming the light from the stars and the moon. A woman and her three dogs scurried down the street. Callie found the house that Jag rented. It sat on a corner lot and overlooked the sound. It had to be the most prime piece of real estate in the entire neighborhood.

She stood behind one of the lampposts, her silhouette stretching tall in the street, but the shadows keeping her identity hidden.

"Boo," a male voice said.

She jumped, dropping her cup and spilling her wine down the front of her shirt. "Fuck," she muttered.

"That's what you get for spying on me," Jag said.

"I wasn't spying. I just went for a walk."

"Really? You just happened to be staying on Whidbey Island, not the mainland."

"You know I've always loved it out here, especially the Saratoga Inn."

"Okay, but explain lurking in front of my house and stopping under the light at the corner of my street, staring into my picture window? I ain't buying it."

"I don't give a fuck," she said, wiping off the dampness from her shirt the best she could. "I didn't even know you lived here."

He tossed his head back and laughed. "Don't lie. It's never been a good look on you. Now, do you want to come in for a drink? Or do you want to go back where you came from?"

"I'll choose the latter," she said, but only because she wasn't ready to have a deeper and longer conversation with the elusive but insanely sexy Jagar Bowie. She'd save that talk for tomorrow when she waltzed into his office with her pad and paper. "Now, if you'll excuse me, I'm going to finish my walk."

"Be safe, Callie," he said. He waved his hand over his head and jogged up the hill toward his house. He paused at the front door. "Take care."

"You too." She turned and headed back toward the Saratoga Inn. Convincing him to help her would take some doing, but she wouldn't quit.

She couldn't.

Not until her sister's murderer was brought to justice.

2

Jag snagged his mug of steaming hot coffee along with Callie's book and made his way to his front porch where he had the most beautiful view of Puget Sound. One of the biggest reasons he was willing to spend a ridiculous amount of money on rent for this prime piece of real estate.

But because he sat on the corner and up high on the hill, he could also see down the road, into town and the Saratoga Inn.

Well, at least one small part of it.

Damn, she looked good. No, great. Better than great. She'd been the most beautiful woman he'd ever laid eyes on and how he ended up engaged to her for less than twenty-four hours he'd never understand. Not only had she been way out of his league, but they couldn't be more different. She was all glitz and glam. She was all about the story, and she'd step on anyone to get it.

Including him.

He was all brawn and ego. All he cared about was the job and having the best record in the department. It meant so much to him that it clouded his judgment and because of that, he couldn't see what was right in front of his face.

Adam Wanton wasn't the Trinket Killer. He couldn't have been. Had Jag been doing his job, he would have questioned the fact that Adam had no trinkets to his name. As a matter of fact, he had a flair for expensive items, and his girlfriend had only the finest of jewelry.

No costume jewelry in her collection anywhere.

But none of that added up to his innocence.

However, the discrepancies in DNA at various crime scenes should have given him pause, but he was too damn fucking excited to wrap up another case.

Seattle's golden boy. That's what people had started calling him, and it had gone to his head.

The dark night sky had started to turn light blue as the sun tried to peek over the horizon. Jag had barely slept a wink. He'd tossed and turned, thinking only of the days and nights he'd had the pleasure of having the magnificent Callie in his arms. He'd fallen head over heels in love with her, and he didn't think he'd ever be able to get her out from under his skin.

Having her back in the Seattle area only made matters worse.

Her asking him for help and him denying her damn near killed him.

He sipped his coffee as he flipped open the book. She'd been extremely kind to him in the pages he'd read so far, which confused him because the title was a huge dig. However, when she got to chapter ten, she did rip him a new one about the arrest.

He made one mistake in procedure by jumping the gun and executing the arrest before the warrant had actually been issued, and she harped on it for eight pages.

Quickly, he flipped to chapter fifteen which discussed all the DNA evidence. The blood evidence that had been gathered at five of the crime scenes, including Stephanie's, that belonged to Adam Wanton had been contaminated. It could have been because the crime scene had been compromised, or it could have been planted there. The thing was, it didn't match the blood at any of the other scenes. That unknown DNA is, in part, what allowed Adam to walk.

But what was even weirder was when Leslie Armstrong, one of the lab techs, admitted to tampering with the samples. Two days later, Leslie killed herself.

Why would she do either of those things?

Of course, Callie believed that Armstrong had been murdered. But by who? It certainly wasn't the Trinket Killer.

Jag had more questions than answers, and this stupid book wasn't helping.

He stared off into the sound, watching the ferry take the next boatload of people into the city. Life on the island was different. It moved at a snail's pace, and Jag had finally begun to settle in and enjoy the lack of adrenaline rush he thought he needed to survive. He never wished anyone to be killed, but a year ago at this time, if there were no murderers, he'd be sitting at his desk twiddling his thumbs, praying for something to happen.

Today, he'd take thumb twiddling any day of the week over a murder investigation. Finding out who stole Jimmy Brendel's bicycle last week was about all the excitement he needed.

He scratched the side of his head.

There had been a slight MO (modus operandi) change halfway through the Trinket Killer murders. It had been Callie who pointed out that the trinkets went from gold to silver. He'd like to believe he would have picked up on it, but if he was being totally honest with himself, he'd started to lose his edge to his ego.

The alarm on his cell went off, alerting him that it was time to head into the office, which was literally almost directly across the street.

He refilled his coffee, locked his door, and headed down the road, leaving Callie's book behind.

Ajax Bond had been instrumental in helping him get the placement as chief of police in the small town of Langley, where he was in charge of four other officers and a population of a little over one thousand citizens. Had it not been for Ajax, Jag might have been fired.

Not for the Trinket Killer case, but for what happened after.

What a shit show.

He pushed open the door to city hall and turned right. "Good morning, Isabelle. How are you? More importantly, how's that little baby of yours?"

"She's doing great, thanks for asking." Isabelle glanced up from the computer screen and smiled like the proud new mommy she was. So young, only twenty-five, but she had a maturity about her, and he was damn glad she decided to keep working. Of course, he would have opened a daycare in city hall to keep her if that's what it took.

"What are you reading this morning?" he asked.

"The *Create the Dew Blob*. The writer is so amazingly adorable. I love her and all her splendid advice." Isabelle leaned forward. "On sex, and trust me, we need all the—"

"Too much information, Isabelle." Jag waved his hands and laughed. Isabelle was always a breath of fresh air, but she often put too much out there. "Looks like we had a quiet night." He redirected the conversation.

"A few speeding tickets, but I should warn you that you do have a visitor in your office," Isabelle said quietly.

He leaned over the desk and glanced through the open door. Fuck. "Why didn't you tell me I had company?"

"You didn't ask," Isabelle said.

"If anyone calls, take a number, and I'll get back to them as soon as possible. Have we done a shift change?"

She nodded. "Jenna just replaced Bo."

"Good to know. Interrupt if there are any emergencies." He made his way into his office, shutting the door behind him. "What are you doing here, Callie?" He didn't bother with the formalities as he set his extra-large travel mug on his desk along with his breakfast sandwich that he'd made at home. What an awesome little kitchen appliance. He could live on egg sandwiches.

"You haven't changed, and I see you're still using my gift," she said.

"Actually, I tossed yours through the window of my old pickup and broke it. I bought a new one."

"You like hurting me, don't you?"

He laughed. "That's rich coming from you. Seriously, Callie, the title for your book is a slap in the face."

"It's not the title I want, and I'm still fighting with the publisher."

"Oh, really. And what do you think the name of the book should be?"

"The Trinket Killer, Still at Large."

"That's a shitty title," he mumbled. Not that he

liked the other much better, but the working title would sell books. That one people wouldn't even use the paperback cover to wipe their ass with. "What about *The Trinket Killer, And How He Got Away With It.*"

"That's actually not bad. I'll run it by the publisher." She tucked her long blond hair behind her ears. It had to have grown a good two inches since the last time he'd seen her. Her dark-brown eyes had lost a bit of their sparkle, but they still had the same determination etched in the rich color.

"I was kidding. I'd prefer you not publish that rubbish at all. I'm sure the Seattle Police Department is giving you some blowback."

She nodded. "There are some things they've forced me to take out, but this is a complicated case, and now that I've had a little time and space from it, I realize how much we both didn't see things."

"I don't need to be reminded of that," he said. "Now, seriously, why are you here?"

She held up her pad of paper and pen. "First, I want to interview you for the book. And second, I want you to investigate the Trinket Killer with me again."

"Well, fuck. And here I thought you might be here to apologize for humiliating me in front of my family, your family, our friends. Hell, the fucking world when you tossed the engagement ring I bought you in my face and called me a murderer on national—"

She held up her hand. "I'm apologizing now."

"I'm going to make this real easy for you. I have no comment on the Trinket Killer or my involvement in it. And if you want help, go to cold cases. I'm sure someone there has been assigned the case, and I'm sure they'd love some help, though you do have quite the reputation for being a bitch."

She tilted her head and pursed her lips. "No thanks to you."

"Oh, for fuck's sake. We could go on like this forever," he said.

She laughed. "We sure did hurt each other, didn't we?"

He leaned back in his chair and clasped his hands behind his head. "That we did, but it's the past, and it's time to let it stay there and move forward."

"Now you sound like Kara. She's doesn't even want to stay on as my researcher for any other true crime books or pieces I do for the network."

He dropped his hands to the desk. "That's

shocking. She was more passionate about the Trinket Killer in the beginning than you were."

"Her wife was the first victim," Callie said. "She made it her life's work, but now she's found love again and wants to put this behind her. That said, I often wonder if the case hadn't gone so cold would she be singing a different tune."

He'd always liked Kara. She stayed in the background, never inserting herself into the thick of the investigation, and when she had an opinion about something, the way she presented it was always professional and in a way that never stepped on anyone's toes.

But she always took Callie's side in any argument, and even more so the moment she found out Callie and Jag were a couple. He thought Kara believed Callie could do better.

Perhaps she could.

"Or maybe you used her to the point she has nothing left to give."

"Wow. You just want to keep on hurting me, don't you?"

"Sorry," he said. "Old habits die hard. But have you ever thought that Stephanie wasn't killed by the Trinket Killer, but a copycat, who also killed Adam?" It was a weak theory but one that had legs.

When Adam had been released from county lockup, he'd disappeared. On the same day, a male body had been found. A few days later, the same day that Stephanie was killed, the male body turned out to be Adam.

Too many coincidences and in his line of work, those didn't exist.

However, that theory was a stretch, and he knew it.

"Of course, I've thought about it," Callie said. "Stephanie had called me a half dozen times the night she was murdered, but you and I were in the middle of getting engaged, so I ignored her calls. Her last message was that she had something important that she had to tell me and you. She sounded desperate and scared."

"I know. I listened to the message a few times. Something definitely had her spooked, and the fact she wanted me there has always made me wonder what upset her."

"Or what she knew. She was desperate to talk to me, but I blew her off." Callie dabbed the corner of her right eye with her shirt, which showed off a little bit of her taut abs.

He shouldn't notice, much less stare. He shifted his gaze upward.

"And then we both got called to a murder, only it was hers," Callie said.

Jag stood and made his way around to the other side of the desk. He sat in the chair next to Callie and took her hands in his. A sizzle crawled across his skin in a blaze of glory. All of his muscles twitched and tightened in preparation for what they remembered having her in his arms meant.

Only it wasn't going to happen.

Not like that.

He was only going to comfort her for a second.

"The one thing I've never actually gotten to say to you without us slinging mud at each other is how truly sorry I am about Stephanie."

"Thank you for that." She gave his hand a good squeeze and pulled away, leaning back in the chair. "I wasn't thinking straight that night. Nor for days after. Hell, I'm not sure my head's been on right since. Even Kara is tired of me and my obsession, but I can't let it go. Stephanie was all the family I had left, and I let her down. I let her down big-time."

He pinched the bridge of his nose and let out a long puff of air. His heart hammered against his ribs. "No. You didn't. But I did," he admitted. "You were right. I fucked up, and I haven't had a good night's sleep since. But for fuck's sake, why do you have to write about it?" He slammed his fist on the desk. Two files jumped right off the surface and landed on the floor.

"I know you've read some of it, or you wouldn't be this mad."

"The title pissed me off enough that I didn't have to open it." He pushed back the chair and gripped the door handle. "I don't know why I thought we could be nice to each other. But we can't. So, I think it's best if you go."

"I can also tell you didn't read the last chapter." She gathered up her things and shoved them in her backpack. "I'll save you the effort." She stood and closed the gap between them. She stood so close he could feel the heat rising off her skin, coating his like a weighted blanket meant to protect, only he felt stifled and unable to move. "Stephanie knew the Trinket Killer."

"Well, duh, we both came to that conclusion at the crime scene," he said with a little more sarcasm than was warranted.

"The Trinket Killer has a type. Women with—"

"Tell me something I don't know, or leave," he said with a dark tone. One of the reasons he couldn't sleep more than an hour or two was because his dreams were haunted with visions of someone murdering Callie. A nightmare he couldn't escape until the Trinket Killer was caught.

Only the bastard had to strike again for that to happen, and it had been a year.

"The crime scene changed subtly three times over the course of twelve murders. The first time had been at murder six when he went from gold to silver trinkets. But I also found that other than my sister, those last victims either wore contacts or glasses. The other victims didn't."

He opened his mouth but snapped it shut. It was an interesting point, one that had been overlooked and could speak to victimology.

"Another pattern I started to notice was height. While all relatively tall and slender, the first girls were all over five six, and some could be a little more curvy than others with larger breasts and all had implants, which was noted but tossed when the trinkets changed."

"It didn't appear relevant at the time, considering I had dead bodies piling up, and some had implants and others didn't. All we knew was pretty young blond women who were professionals."

"Well, the latter victims were closer to five foot five with small breasts, except my sister. My sister didn't fit the current MO. So, either something changed with the Trinket Killer, or my sister stepped in the killer's way."

"Or both," he said with an arched brow. "This is not earth-shattering information."

She pulled out a piece of paper and shoved it in his face. "Do the math, something I didn't even think about a year ago because it wouldn't have made sense to."

He held the timeline of victims and their deaths with all the information she just spewed in his hands. "What the fuck am I looking at, Callie?"

"Victim number six literally happened the night we ran into each other at McCurdy's. The first night we slept together."

"I remember the night, not the day of the week or month." He scratched the side of his head. "And so?"

"I never told you this, but the Trinket Killer contacted me."

He let go of the door handle. His jaw slacked open. "Jesus, Callie. You were fucking the lead detective on the case, and you just don't think to tell him, oh, by the way, I spoke to the killer the other day."

"It wasn't like that, and I didn't actually speak

to the killer, but he left me a couple of notes. They are in the book in the last chapter."

"He contacted you more than once?"

"The first time was after his ninth murder, and the note said: *this one's for him*. At first, I didn't know it was from the killer or what it even meant until he did it again with the next two murders."

"You should have told me," he said. "Those notes could have had prints."

"I had an independent lab—"

"Save the justification. I'm not even sure why I'm standing here listening because I'm not a detective anymore. I'm the chief of police of a very small town where stopping someone for running a red light is the most thrilling part of my day."

She set her purse on the desk and pulled out a plastic envelope. "Okay. Then this will be in your jurisdiction."

"What is it?"

"A note from the Trinket Killer that was left in front of my door at the Saratoga Inn this morning."

3

Callie sat in the living room of the Saratoga Inn, hugging her purse. She stared out the big picture window at the slight drizzle misting from the sky. The thin fog rolled through the hills and out to the sound.

"Here you go." Kara handed her a Diet Coke before sitting in the chair next to her. "What exactly did the note say?"

"Welcome back, Callie. I've got a trinket or two for you. Let the games begin." Callie shivered.

"I wish you would have called me the second you found the note."

"I didn't feel like hearing, I told you coming back to Seattle was a mistake." Callie chugged half the can of soda. She needed a good boost of caffeine if she was going to get through a day with Jag in detective mode. It amazed her how quickly he went from the new laid-back, relaxed Jag to his old in charge, barking out orders at a crime scene Jag.

"Seattle has too many ghosts for both of us. It's making me crazy too, and I ended up fighting with Ivy last night."

"Over what?" Callie asked. Kara had been just as obsessed with the Trinket Killer as Callie, but in a different way. Kara's wife had been the first known victim, and when Callie had first met Kara, it seemed all Kara wanted was knowledge and to help in some small way.

That's how she ended up being her research assistant, and she'd been a damn good one for the most part. She'd never been trained in the field, so there were some skills she lacked, but she was a fast learner, and Callie trusted her, which was huge because she didn't trust too many people.

"Being back here brings up a lot of memories and feelings over Renee, and while Ivy isn't jealous of my late wife, she does get upset over the obsession that begins when we walk into this city."

"She used the word we?"

Kara nodded.

"I'm sorry." The last thing Callie wanted to do was ruin anyone's relationship. Kara and Ivy had only been together for about five months, but Callie had seen a huge change in Kara's well-being since she'd fallen in love. It was good for Kara after all these years to move on.

"It's not your fault." Kara reached out and took Callie's hand. "It's mine, but knowing that killer is out there, lurking in the streets of Seattle, makes me want to run."

Callie nodded. Before her sister died, it had just been another story. Another notch on her career belt. She was hungry to make a name for herself.

Now it was all about making sure her sister didn't die in vain.

"Besides, that note sounded more like a threat," Kara said. "Why didn't you tell me you were staying out here?"

"I didn't want a lecture about Jag."

Kara laughed. "Other than Jag being an arrogant asshole, I think he's a good guy. But he did fuck up the case, and seriously, we both know they caught the wrong guy, but he just wouldn't listen. He's a stubborn mule, and to be honest, I wish anyone but him was handling this now."

"You don't like him because he accused you of killing your wife, but statistically—"

"Hey, he was the first one to apologize when I was cleared, so he gets points for that. I just wish you weren't still so hung up on him. He's not worth it."

Callie wished the same thing. Falling in love with Jag had been the most unexpected thing that had ever happened. Of all the men she'd met, Jag wasn't even on her radar. Sure, she'd found him sexy when they had crossed paths, but they butted heads in ways that wasn't conducive to even having a conversation.

Until that night at the bar.

A heated discussion turned into a night of passion that didn't end until the Trinket Killer murdered their love for one another.

"I'm over him, but he's a damn good cop. Everyone makes mistakes, and sadly, I'm as much to blame for that botched investigation as he was, and my sister is dead because of it."

"Oh, stop that right now," Kara said. "There is only one person responsible for Stephanie's murder, and that's the Trinket Killer. So stop that self-destructive thinking. I'm really tired of it."

Callie patted Kara's thigh. She'd been her rock

for the last year. Kara had stuck by Callie's side during her darkest moments. Her friendship meant everything. However, it was time for Kara to take the next step. "I think you and Ivy should leave now. I appreciate both of you coming back here, but I don't want this to be the cause of problems between you two."

"I'm glad you feel that way because I told Ivy this morning that we can go back to San Francisco. We were going to leave today, but we can wait until—"

"No. Go now. Get on the next ferry and get the hell out of this godforsaken place. Whatever work we need to finish for the book, you can do from your place in San Fran."

"Are you sure? I wouldn't go, but I want to make this work with Ivy."

Callie smiled. "Ivy's amazing. You should go."

"Thank you." Kara leaned in and hugged Callie. She held Kara for a long moment, resting her head on her shoulder.

The sound of someone clearing his throat startled her.

"Oh, hey there, Jag," Kara said as she stood, stretching out her hand. "You look like hell as usual."

"And you're still the prettiest woman in any room." He took her hand and pulled her in for a brief hug, giving her a little peck on the cheek.

"Even if I was interested in men, which I'm not, I'd be way out of your league."

"Most women are," he said with a chuckle.

"I'll talk to you later," Kara said as she headed for the front door.

"Text me when you get to San Fran." Callie didn't bother to stand up. It wasn't even noon, and she felt like she'd put in a full day already.

"Why is she going there?" Jag asked.

"It's where she and her girlfriend live and honestly, there are too many ghosts for her in this city."

"Understandable." He pointed to her bag. "Let's go get something to eat, and then you can come back here and pack up your stuff."

"Why would I pack up my stuff? I have this place booked for a month. The publisher wants extra chapters and a few other things that need to be tweaked."

"I've got a better view at my place, and I work twelve-hour days. You'll have all the peace and quiet you'll need."

"I'm not staying with you." She stood and

tossed her backpack over her shoulder. "I'll move into the motel down the street."

"Like hell. That would be even less secure."

She followed him down the steps of the Saratoga Inn and around the corner into town and Michaels, a quaint little seaside diner that made the best crab cake sandwich she'd ever had. "Slow down and stop being such a Neanderthal."

He glanced over his shoulder, pointing an angry finger at the inn. "You're not staying there alone. Or anywhere else for that matter. I have a spare bedroom. So, until I catch that fucking bastard once and for all, you're staying with me, and that's the end of it."

God, she hated it when he went all alpha male macho sexist pig on her. It wasn't sweet or endearing, and even though she knew his heart was in the right place, because deep down, he was a good man and at one time, he cared for her deeply, it still annoyed the hell out of her. "You're not my daddy, so you can't make me."

"Watch me." He opened the door to the diner and gave her a little shove.

Of course the place was packed. The hostess raced over with a big smile. "Hi, Jag. There is a table out front if you don't mind sitting outside.

The sun is trying to peek out, and it's not drizzling at all anymore."

"Does that work for you?" He turned his head and glared at Callie.

She touched the center of her chest. "Oh, this I get an opinion about?"

"Not really. We'll take the table," he said, and taking her hand, he led her through the restaurant to the outside patio.

Seagulls soared overhead, looking for easy food. A few boats filled the sound as the sun tried to create the warmth of spring. She zipped up her fleece. It wasn't quite there yet, so she was grateful there was no breeze coming off the sound.

She took the seat with her back to the diner so she could look out over the water and enjoy the view. She and Jag had spent many lazy afternoons at this place when they'd managed a day off at the same time. They'd come out here to be away from the hustle and bustle of the city.

They also wanted to keep their relationship to themselves. At first, it had been because it was just sex.

But then it was because they were both utterly terrified of what was happening.

However, about three months before they got engaged, it became a game of how to tell people. They told Stephanie first. The look of shock and horror had been classic, and it had Jag rolling on the floor laughing. But once Stephanie spent time with the two of them, she could see the love they had for one another.

Jag waved his hand in front of Callie's face. "Where'd you go?"

"Sorry, I was thinking about Stephanie." No point in lying.

"Yeah," he said softly. "But we need to discuss that note."

The waitress stepped in front of the table, thankfully taking their order and giving her a few more minutes to collect her thoughts.

"Why didn't you call me the second you saw that note? Instead, you compromised evidence. That makes my job harder, and you of all people know that."

"I told you before that it was on my continental breakfast tray, tucked under a plate. I didn't see it right away. I actually didn't open the envelope until I was halfway out the door to see you."

"That doesn't answer the question of why you didn't tell me about it the second you saw me. Or better yet, tell my secretary so she could have called one of my officers on duty."

She tossed her hands wide. "I don't know. Call me Nancy Drew."

"Okay, Nancy Drew."

"You've always loved to mock me. Anyway, old habits die hard. And honestly, don't you think it's a little strange that I'm not even in town for more than a couple of days and all of a sudden the Trinket Killer decides to say hello?"

"Actually, I do think that's odd, considering we haven't heard from him in a year."

"It might not be him."

"Might not be, but someone slipped into the Saratoga Inn, wiped the security footage, and left a threatening note that basically said he was going to start killing again. Now maybe it's a copycat. Maybe it's someone who wants to fuck with you. Or me. Or both of us. But you look an awful lot like every single girl who was murdered, and I'm not going to let anything happen to you on my watch."

"What about every other long-haired blond who—"

"Don't be like that," he said with a harsh tone. "I'm doing what I can. You saw the CSI team, and they are dusting for prints and going through that room with a fine-tooth comb."

"Why aren't you there controlling their every move?"

"My officer Jenna graduated top of her class. If her husband wasn't deployed half the year and she didn't have two little kids, she'd be living in Seattle working Vice or Homicide. She's going to head up your case."

"Are you kidding me? You're pawning something on someone else?"

He tapped the badge that hung on his shirt. "I'm the chief. It's my job to play more of a supervisory role. Besides, I'm not the arrogant dickhead I used to be. I know when I'm too close and need to back off." He opened his napkin and spread it out across his lap. "You, on the other hand, can't get out of your own way. Your book proves it."

She leaned back and smiled. "So, you did read it."

"I plead the fifth."

Jag took his cell and his beer and headed to the front porch. He glanced over his shoulder at Callie, who had her headphones on and her face only a few inches from her laptop screen.

"Hey, sis." He sat in his favorite chair, resting his legs on the coffee table as he watched the sky grow dark.

"Are you out of your freaking mind?" Ziggy's voice screeched in his ear.

He adjusted the volume on his AirPods. "You don't have to yell."

"Oh, someone does. I can't believe you are having her move in with you, and you didn't even have the decency to call me to tell me she was back."

"She's not living with me. I'm letting her stay in my guest room for a bit." He chuckled. Ziggy had a flair for the dramatic and tended to overreact.

Hell, that had been a problem for most of his family, including him, though he always told himself he acted and never reacted, but as he approached his mid-thirties, he could see the error of his ways. What he thought was taking action often never gave his mind a chance to process important information that would later come back and bite him in the ass.

Like waiting until he got the phone call from Ajax that the judge signed off on all arrest and search warrants before executing them, and he only needed that because they didn't have probable cause. He had no reason to pick Adam up. Everything had been on a hunch until the DNA came back.

He blinked, pushing all those thoughts from his brain.

"Why is she back anyway?" Ziggy asked.

"To finish her book."

"I can't believe she's using that title. It makes you look bad," Ziggy said with a huff.

Of everyone in his family, Ziggy had taken the news of his relationship with Callie better than most. Ziggy worked for the same station as a producer. They butted heads a lot, but mostly because they had similar personalities, yet they were also friends.

However, they both had one fatal flaw. Neither one of them knew how to let things go.

"The book isn't as bad as I thought, as long as she can get the publisher to change the title. It appears that's more of a marketing ploy than anything else."

"Are you saying she no longer blames you? Because I know deep down she never meant those things she said. She couldn't have. She loves you."

He pinched the bridge of his nose. He wanted to believe that Callie didn't blame him for Stephanie's death, but she did hold him responsible for mistakes.

And for not listening to her.

And she wouldn't be wrong for doing so. "If she loved me, she wouldn't have tossed my engagement ring at my head on live television and all but call me a murderer."

"She was grieving."

This argument was getting old, and he needed to stop entertaining the dialogue. "You didn't call me to discuss my living arrangement with Callie."

"That was part of it. How is she?"

That caught a hearty laugh. "Seriously? You can't burn that candle at both ends. When she left, you told me your friendship was over."

"I was mad and hurt. I'm over it," Ziggy said. "Is she still totally obsessed?"

"Pretty much," he admitted. "But in a different way. Once Stephanie was murdered, this became personal. There is a sadness about her that wasn't there before."

"It's only been a year. Grief is a tricky thing," Ziggy said. "And now on to the other reason I called. I wanted to warn you that our newest greedy little up-and-coming reporter is going to be coming out there tomorrow morning to get an interview from you and Callie."

Why was he surprised. He took a double swig of his beer. The bubbles tickled his nose. "I thought Callie was bad, but Bailey would toss her mother under the bus for a story."

"Thank God I'm not her producer," Ziggy said. "Now do me a favor and don't let anything happen to Callie."

His boots hit the wood floor. "Why did you just say that?" There had been no news crew. No reporters. No one knew he'd called CSI. Hell, the few things that happened out on Whidbey were never worth the evening news. But anytime his sister got cryptic, it usually meant there was buzz around her work water cooler.

And that was never good for him.

"Bailey got a tip that Callie is staying at the Saratoga Inn and that her room was broken into and that you called for extra help from the mainland."

Well, that wasn't what happened. He began making a mental note of everyone he'd seen at the inn. He'd need to get a guest list, and he'd need to make sure that Ronnie, the owner, didn't say anything to the press. "I can't comment."

"I don't expect you to," Ziggy said. "I do know that Bailey plans on starting with Callie."

"How does she expect to find her since she's no longer at the inn?"

"Funny you should ask," Ziggy said. "Her anonymous source said to try your place."

"Fucking wonderful," he mumbled. "Thanks for the warning."

"You're welcome. Watch your back."

"Love you, Ziggy."

"Love you too, brother."

He tapped his AirPods and pulled them from his ears.

"Want another beer?" Callie eased into the chair next to him, handing him a longneck.

"Fuck, you scared me," he said, taking the cold beverage. "How long have you been standing there?"

"Long enough to know that Ziggy is still the best, and Bailey is still a little bitch who got her wish since she's now in my job."

He raised his beer and clanked it against the one in Callie's hand. "She's not half as good as you were."

She chuckled. "Since when do you toss around compliments like they are candy."

He shrugged.

"Any news from the lab?" she asked.

"Too many prints so it's all compromised. And the note is clean, except your prints."

"I can't believe no one saw anything," she said.

"Well, the good news is that the art gallery right behind the inn has a security camera that faces the back of the inn. There is a shadow of a person running out the back at around five in the morning."

"So, whoever it was had to have taken a ferry over yesterday."

"No. They could have driven over the deception pass bridge. Or they could have already been here." He rested his head against the cushion and stared at the sky. He found a couple of stars, and the white moon glowed through a thin layer of gray clouds. "I'm taking this threat seriously, which is why I am being a bit of a dick by having you stay here, but I don't think it's the Trinket Killer."

"I have to agree. You are being a dick."

He chuckled. "But you're staying."

"Just for a couple of nights. Because it's so

pretty here and the motel down the street doesn't have anything until Monday."

"I can't force you to stay, but someone wants us to think the Trinket Killer is watching us and ready to strike again."

"What if he is? What if me being back in Seattle is some kind of trigger? What if I just set in motion another killing spree?"

Jag had to admit, at least to himself, that those same questions filled his mind, but it didn't make sense if he pulled it back to the beginning. "What were you doing when the first murder took place?"

"What do you mean?"

"You were a junior reporter, and you didn't even cover that case. I was a beat cop. I had just taken my detective test, but it was a full year before I got my first case."

"Which was the fourth victim," she said. "And that was the second murder I covered."

"I know. You pissed me off when you gave the killer a name and then publicly made the connection between a couple of the murders before we were ready to make that announcement."

"People have the right to know there is a serial killer in the neighborhood, but I now see how I went too far sometimes."

"You were just doing your job," he said.

"Wow. Who are you, and what did you do with my ex-fiancé?"

He spit out half his beer as he burst out laughing. "We were engaged for less than a day, and I don't think I've ever heard you use that word and my name in the same sentence."

"It did feel very weird on my tongue."

"Don't turn your head or anything, but we've got company," he said.

"Who? Where?"

"I don't know. I don't recognize the car, but someone is definitely sitting in it. Without causing alarm, I want you to quickly go inside."

"What are you going to do?"

"Call my officer on duty. I always have two. And have them do a sweep while I sit here with my gun." He pulled it out of its holster and put it on the table. "And watch."

"I'll be inside." She scurried through the front door, shutting it quickly. At least she didn't argue. That was a change from the days of the past. She always had to be in the thick of things. Right there with him on the front lines. The story meant more to her than anything else, including him.

But who was he to talk? She often took a back seat to his job.

He stuffed his AirPods back in his ear. "Hey Siri, call Jenna Earls."

It rang once. "Hey, Chief. What's up?"

"Are you in your patrol car?"

"Yup. Just sitting up at the corner by the motel, waiting to get someone for a rolling stop."

He laughed. "I need you to drive down to my neighborhood and check out a car parked just at the bend by my house."

"Be there in five."

He tapped his phone but left the earpiece in while he pretended to kick back and enjoy his second beer. Which actually felt really good as it bubbled down his esophagus and into his stomach.

Headlights cut through the dark night.

The car in question flicked its lights on and eased down the road.

His cell buzzed.

"Hey, Jenna," he said.

"I've got the plate, and I'm running it now. Do you want me to follow... Well, now, that's interesting."

"What?"

"The car is registered to Bailey Redding."

"Of course it is," he said. "Yeah. Follow her. Find out if she's staying here on the island and if you can come up with a reason to pull her over, do it."

"She's got a taillight out."

"Perfect. Feel free to give her a ticket," he said. "We need to feed the beast that all women cops are bitches."

"God, you're such an asshole," she said with a laugh.

He'd known Jenna for years. They went through the academy together and for a short time were partners as beat cops. They didn't come any better than Jenna.

"I won't argue that point," he said before ending the call. He finished his beer. Time to head inside and try to get some sleep.

It was going to be hard with Callie in his house.

Worse, because she wouldn't be in his bed.

4

Callie leaned against the porch railing and looked out over the sound. Life on Whidbey Island seemed to slow to a snail's pace. A year ago, she could only tolerate that for a day, maybe two. Now, she thought she might like to live this way for the rest of her life.

The view alone soothed her aching heart. His house sat up on the hill in the back of the neighborhood and looked out over everyone else. It was if the chief of police was actually keeping an eye on his citizens.

One of his neighbors walked down the street with a dog in tow. She glanced up and waved with a puzzled expression.

Small towns.

People would be talking, but she suspected Seattle was already abuzz about her return. She might not be famous, but she certainly left an impression, and the video still occasionally made the rounds on social media.

She blew into the oversized mug. She'd managed to make a pot of coffee without blowing anything up. She had horrible luck with appliances. Back in the day, she'd broken so many of Jag's gadgets that he banned her from his kitchen.

"Good morning, sunshine."

She jumped, sloshing her coffee all down the front of her white pajama shirt. "Mother trucker."

"Yeah. That's not coming out."

"Probably not, so let's be glad I stole this shirt from you."

He raced inside and quickly returned with a small towel, pressing it against her chest.

She held the half-empty cup to the side and glared at him. "Really? Are you done feeling me up?"

"They're a little bigger than they used to be."

Snagging the towel, she twirled it and whipped it at his shoulder. "Asshole."

"Ouch, that hurt."

"Good," she muttered, wishing that she didn't enjoy the banter. Their relationship had always been one of yin and yang. Tit for tat. Their world views were identical, but how they approached everything couldn't be more opposite. It made for some pretty intense conversations that turned into passionate lovemaking sessions.

"Guess who managed to get my cell," she said.

He laughed. "Oh, let me take a wild stab at that one." He tapped his foot and raised his hand, flicking his index finger against his temple. "The pope?"

"Haha, funny guy."

He laughed. "I take it you mean Bailey. Did you answer? Respond?"

She shook her head. "She left a message last night at nine thirty, asking me to call her first thing. She wants to meet me for an informal late lunch or early cocktail to discuss the possibility of doing a sit-down interview in the studio about the book."

"Are you going to meet her?"

Callie took the last sip of coffee and set the mug on the railing. She folded her arms across her chest. The wet shirt clung to her skin, sending a slight shiver across her body. The temperature was in the seventies, which was unseasonably warm for May in Seattle, but she'd enjoy every second of it. In a few hours, things might be gray, misty, and cold, like usual. "I'm planning on it, but I have no intention of doing an on-camera interview. Not now anyway, and not with her."

"If you did do one, who would it be with?"

"Jackie from Channel 8," she said without hesitation. In all of Callie's career, her biggest competition for ratings had been Jackie Cash.

"Wow. She used to drive you crazy."

"Only when she got the story before I did," Callie admitted. "Those days are over, but Bailey is a backstabbing bitch and with how she handled the coverage of my sister's murder and our breakup by putting them up on her social media to use as her first big break into reporting, well, I don't want to give her shit. Jackie and I were always professional with each other."

"Yeah, Jackie's not so bad." He laughed, shaking his head. "I took her out a few months ago."

"I never needed to know that," Callie said.

"Then maybe you don't want to know I also took out Bailey."

"Gross." She held her stomach. "Why would

you do that? Jackie I can maybe understand. But Bailey?"

"Yeah. She was a mistake. Rebound to get over you. But Jackie was different."

"I don't want to hear this."

"Are you jealous?" He winked.

"Maybe a little, but only because they are both in the same profession, and before you and I hooked up, you used to say, and I quote, '*Reporters and journalists are the devil. Wait. Nope. They are worse. They are the armpit of the earth.*'"

He burst out laughing. "I did say that. And if it makes you feel any better, the date with Jackie didn't even get off the ground. We ordered drinks and an appetizer, and before we ordered a meal, she was like, you're a jerk."

"What did you do? Make some sexist joke?" She shook her head. "I've never understood why you do that when you're really the furthest thing from a misogynistic pig."

"Actually, I was a perfect gentleman. The problem was I couldn't stop talking about you. I guess I wasn't ready to start dating again."

"Are you dating now?" she asked.

He shook his head. "No. You?"

"I don't have the time with a deadline looming. Speaking of which, I need to know if—"

"You will never get an interview from me for that book, just so we're clear on that."

She figured as much, but she realized that since she'd been back in town, she'd never done the one thing he deserved most. "You've been really kind to me since I returned."

"I don't know about that. Had you not been threatened, I'm not sure I would have given you the time of day."

"I'm sorry." Tentatively, she took a few tiny steps forward. "I said a lot of hurtful things to you at my sister's crime scene and again at home. And what I did to you on national television, well, it was just uncalled for, and if I could go back in time, I'd do that all differently."

"But you'd still give me my ring back."

She reached out and cupped his cheek with her palm. "Considering everything, it was for the best."

He curled his fingers around her wrist. "I appreciate the apology."

"I had to blame someone that I could see, feel, and touch. The Trinket Killer was either dead or nowhere to be found. You were standing right in front of me. You had lied to me, and I didn't feel like I could trust you."

"We lied to each other, and for the record, I had to. I couldn't tell you those things we were keeping from the public and the press. I was on thin ice as it was because you always seemed to be one step ahead of all the other reporters." He pulled her to his chest. "And let's not forget you hacked into my computer and read reports you shouldn't have. That's criminal, and I could have—"

"I know. And I'm sorry. I wish I hadn't done that and I never used that information." She closed her eyes for a long moment. "Until I tossed my engagement ring at you in front of the world."

"I'm lucky I have a job, and you're lucky you're not in jail." He wrapped his arms around her waist, forcing her to rest her hands on his strong shoulders.

"We both made a lot of mistakes." She tilted her head and stared into his deep dark eyes. A year ago, she thought she couldn't live without him. He'd been everything she wanted in a man.

Or so she thought.

It still hurt that he hadn't listened to her theories about the Trinket Killer. She knew it might not have saved her sister, but she'd never know because he never looked into it.

"What are you trying to get out of this book?" His hands gently roamed up and down her back, massaging her tight muscles. To be in his arms again felt like she'd come home. Her brain told her to take a step back and protect her soul.

Her heart had other ideas and didn't seem to care that it would soon be bleeding out on the floor if she caved to any of her desires.

She clasped her fingers together behind his neck. "Closure."

"We may never find the killer."

"Have you totally stopped looking? Have you given up completely?"

"No," he whispered as he pressed his mouth against hers in a sweet kiss. He tasted like a combination of bitter coffee and cinnamon. His tongue eased between her lips, igniting a fire that started in her toes and slithered across her body like a snake, hitting every erogenous zone, ensuring her knees went weak.

His hands cupped her ass, heaving her even closer.

She raised up on tiptoe, ignoring the little voice

in the back of her head telling her that this was a bad idea.

But it felt so good.

So right.

But it's wrong, said that damn voice.

"Jag," she said, sliding her hand down his taut pectoral muscles. She moaned.

He raised her hand and kissed her palm. "I need to go shower. I have to be at the office in a half hour. I left you a set of keys on the kitchen table. Promise me you'll keep me up to date on your whereabouts? I'm taking that note seriously, and if I had the manpower, I'd have someone on your tail twenty-four seven."

"Other than meeting Bitch Bailey, I plan on staying right here on this front porch and working."

He pointed to the corner of the house. "Just an FYI. I've got cameras covering all entrances."

"And inside your home?"

"Just in your shower." He chuckled. "I'm kidding. I have no cameras inside. I left you a detailed sheet with internet and all that on the table. You can call me if you need me. I'll drive by when I'm on patrol." He kissed her nose, and with that, he turned on his heel and left her standing there with her fingers on her lips, wondering what the hell just happened.

Callie sat on the rooftop of Georgio's Bar and Grill and stared out over the water. She could get used to this kind of life, only she would definitely miss fast food, since about the only place you could find that on the island was at the ferry depot.

And that wasn't the kind of fast food she craved.

She glanced at her watch. God, she hated it when people were late. When she worked as reporter and journalist, she always made sure she was at least five to ten minutes early for any prearranged meeting.

She pulled out the paper copy of the manuscript and a pen. She might as well make good use of the time.

The waitress pushed through the door and headed in her direction. "Are you sure I can't get you anything while you wait?"

"Yeah. I'll take a glass of your house Pinot Grigio. The nine ounce." Normally, Callie wouldn't dare think of having a glass of wine before five, but screw it. Three in the afternoon wasn't that far off.

Getting through any meeting with the likes of Bailey would require taking the edge off.

"I'll be right back with that."

"As I live and breathe," a male voice said.

She turned her head. "Holy shit. Is that little boy Zane Piece?" She stood and gave Zane a hug. "I still hate you for your hair."

Zane's brother happened to be Jag's cousin from his mother's side of the family.

He ran a hand through his long, thick hair. "Darcie told me you were back in town."

"What did Jag's little sister have to say about my book?"

"Nothing good," Zane said. "Are you meeting Jag?"

She shook her head. "I have a meeting. What about you? On a hot date?"

"My girlfriend bailed." He sighed. "Seems to be a thing lately. Just as well. The club called and they are short-staffed."

"So, you're still working at Club Allure. What is that like? I mean it's got to be weird when random people that you know show up at a sex club."

"Not really." He kissed her cheek. "Maybe we can have lunch or something. I'd love to catch up."

"Sounds great."

No sooner did Zane disappear than Bailey burst onto the rooftop with her perfectly styled shoulder-length dark hair. "So sorry I'm late. We're doing a piece on the distillery, and we went over a little."

"So, your camera crew is with you?"

Bailey nodded. "They are getting burgers down the street. I didn't want you to think I was going back on my word." She adjusted her chair and tucked a piece of hair behind her ear. "It's so good to see you again."

Callie couldn't say the same, but she'd do the fake bullshit ex-coworker thing because there was no point not to. "You as well," she said. "I've caught a few of your reports over the last few months. You've settled in nicely."

"Thanks. Your shoes were tough to fill."

Of course they were. Oh, she really needed to stop being so resentful. The girl was just doing her job. Something Callie used to do and not much differently.

"I want to make sure all of this is off the record," Callie said just as the waitress reappeared, setting her glass of wine in front of her. She actually wished she hadn't ordered it now. Especially when Bailey ordered a sparkling water. They both ordered the salad special.

"Full disclosure. We're doing a piece on your return whether you like it or not," Bailey said.

"Why am I not surprised," she said with a sarcastic laugh, shoving the manuscript back into her bag.

"There's a lot of buzz now that you're back and a lot of discussion about the book deal. I have a conference call with your publisher and editor. Your agent hasn't returned my call. I was hoping you'd be able to facilitate that."

"I'm sorry, but I'll be asking my agent not to speak to you. That said, I'm sure my publisher will enjoy the publicity." Bad press was better than no press. She lifted the wineglass to her lips and took a good gulp. "Let me give you a little piece of advice. When dealing with someone who doesn't want anything on record, don't come out of the gate with both barrels loaded. You've basically told me that anything I say might as well be used against me."

"Oh no," Bailey said. "I'm sorry if I came off too aggressively, because that wasn't my intention at all. I will only use what I've gathered on my own, which is all public, and what your publisher tells me. People are curious, though, as to what you've been up to."

"I've been writing a book," she said matter-of-factly.

"There are a lot of rumors around about the title of the book and how that might affect your fiancé."

Callie let out a dry laugh. She wanted to tell Bailey that they knew she'd been the one sitting outside of Jag's house last night, but instead, she'd rather fuck with the little pain in the ass reporter. "He's my ex-fiancé, and I'm still working with the publisher on the title. I actually sent them over a few more ideas this morning."

"Care to share?"

"I do not," she said.

"Can't blame a girl for trying." A short silence filled the air while the waitress refilled their waters and set their salads on the table.

Bailey leaned across the table. Her gaze darted left and right as if she were checking to make sure no one was paying attention. "This isn't my place, but you're so much better off without Jag. He's such an asshole."

"Really? And what makes you say that?"

Bailey cocked her head. "Well, I don't like to talk about it, but he and I had a short thing a while ago. I had to end it because of what an arrogant dirtbag he is, but you know that."

"Actually, I don't because he and I didn't break up for any other reason than my sister was murdered and I was in pain and I needed someone to blame. I chose him, but it wasn't his fault." *Now use that in your local piece, bitch.* "And this isn't why I came here. So, Bailey, tell me. What's the angle with this piece? What are you going to focus on?"

Bailey narrowed her eyes and pursed her lips. She leaned back and smoothed out her hair, letting out a long breath. "Unfortunately, your return has stirred up a lot of raw emotions for a lot of people, including family members of other victims."

"That's bullshit. I've spoken to almost all of them over the last year. They've been amazing with my research for the book. I've become very close to some, and I doubt I'm causing an uproar with them."

"What about Kara? She split pretty quickly. Why's that?" Bailey dug into her salad. Ruthless was the only way to describe her. "Was it just too much for her to be back in Seattle?"

Callie's stomach churned. "I won't speak for Kara."

"Fair enough." Bailey waved her fork in the air. "Why did you come back to Seattle?"

If Bailey was going to do a piece on her regardless, Callie might as well direct it as much as possible.

"I came back mostly to finish the book."

"What's missing?"

Callie chuckled. "Nothing, really. The publisher just wanted some fine-tuning, especially about my sister, and I thought it would be best if I came back to where it all started."

"It's got to be hard for you to have to constantly relive it. I'm not sure I could," Bailey said.

"I don't have a choice." Callie took another gulp of her wine. Drinking on a partially empty stomach wasn't a good idea. She waved at the waitress and pointed to her glass. "My sister was murdered, and that's a fact I can't change. Her killer has never been caught, nor has he killed again, that we know of. A day doesn't go by that I don't think about all the victims and their families."

"And how do you think your book is going to help them?"

"It keeps the memory of their loved ones alive. They don't become another statistic in a cold case sitting in some basement somewhere totally forgotten. It keeps this case relevant."

"I suppose it does, since everyone now wants an interview with you and Chief Bowie."

"This isn't about me or Jag. It's about the victims and their families. That's your story."

"That brings me to a question that is burning on everyone's lips," Bailey said.

"Yeah, what's that?"

"Are you going to ask for your old job back?"

Callie bit down on her tongue to stop from laughing. All this chick cared about was herself and her job. "I have no desire to be a reporter anymore."

"Good to know." She glanced at her watch. "Crap. I've got to go." She glanced over her shoulder.

"I'll take care of the bill," Callie said.

"Thanks. I really appreciate it. I hope when you see the piece we're doing that you'll change your mind and do a sit-down with me at the station. Take care." Bailey took off so fast you'd think the building was on fire.

The waitress showed up with her second glass of wine. "Can I have a piece of chocolate cake?"

"You sure can," the waitress said.

"Thank you." She pulled out her phone and smiled.

Kara: *Hey, Callie girl, just wanted you to know we stopped in Medford, Oregon, and are going to stay for a few days. I hate to say it, but just being back in Seattle did me in.*

Callie: *Enjoy your travels. You and Ivy deserve it.*

Kara: *Thanks! And remember, when you're done there, you've always got a place to lay your head with us.*

Callie: *Love you.*

Kara: *Right back at you.*

As much as Callie missed Kara, she was happy Kara had been able to let go of her own obsession with the Trinket Killer and was able to find love again.

Too bad that would never happen for Callie. She touched her lips. Kissing him again was like having a little taste of what heaven might be like. She'd never be able to love anyone the way she loved him. She didn't think she'd ever be able to get over him. Being back in Seattle proved that.

Her phone buzzed.

Jag: *Where are you?*

Callie: *On my second glass of wine at Georgio's and about to dig into their chocolate cake.*

Jag: *Day drinking and cake? That must have been a shitty meeting.*

Callie: *You have no idea.*

Jag: *I get off work in an hour. Do you want me to come get you? Or will you be okay to walk home?*

She chuckled. Getting good and drunk right about now sounded like a really good idea.

Callie: *I'm going to get two pieces of cake to go and get a bottle from the store. I'll see you at home.*

Jag: *Home? That's very Freudian. Haha.*

She rolled her eyes.

As much as she enjoyed being around him again, for the sake of her heart, she needed to get out of his house, even if it meant she went back to the mainland.

5

One of the nice things about being the chief of police was that for the most part, he got to keep bankers' hours.

Well, that's the lie he told himself.

If he wasn't in the office or on the streets, he was doing the one thing he promised his parents, two sisters, and one brother that he wouldn't do and that was obsess over the Trinket Killer.

He tried to stop investigating, but it proved to be impossible. The cold case detectives gave him monthly updates, which consisted of: *sorry man, we've got nothing.* Jag spent every morning before he went to the office staring at twelve dead girls and every night before he went to bed doing the same thing.

He constantly looked over his shoulder, waiting for the Trinket Killer to show his ugly face.

He leaned back in his chair and clasped his hands behind his back. His home office he kept under lock and key. If anyone in his family saw it, they'd have him committed.

If Callie saw his victim wall, she'd be pulling him knee-deep into her book, and he just wasn't ready to do that. Neither one of them had been able to uncover anything new. It was as if the killer was sitting back, watching them and laughing at their inability to solve this one.

He stood and planted his hands on his hips, rolling his right hand over his weapon. He let out a long breath and inched closer to the wall. Besides their obvious similarities in appearance, there was nothing else to connect them to each other. Not one victim knew the other.

Four were lesbians. One considered herself bisexual.

And then there was Stephanie, born Steven.

She'd gone through her transition years ago but didn't have the surgery until a year before her murder, and according to Callie, she hadn't been happier. She even had a girlfriend, though a secret one.

One who she'd never introduced to Callie, or even given her name.

That shouldn't come as such a shock to him considering how long he and Callie managed to keep their relationship out of the public eye. However, their families knew months before Stephanie's death.

But both Callie and he agreed, even in a drunken stupor, that Stephanie's girlfriend had something to do with her death.

He turned and tapped at the keyboard in front of his computer, pulling up the FBI profile report. His captain had asked him to call in the Feds for support after the eighth murder. He did so willingly and absolutely believed their assessment.

The unsub is most likely a white male, approximately between thirty and forty years of age. He's organized and highly educated. It is not sexually motivated. There is no rape or any mutilation of the body. The unsub is targeting a specific type of woman. Because he leaves the same trinket behind, we believe these women remind him of someone. That he is killing the same woman over and over again.

Pretty standard stuff.

But because they didn't notice the change from gold to silver with the trinket, and perhaps they missed other things, this profile wasn't viable anymore.

The sound of footsteps coming down the stairs caught his attention. Quickly, he locked the door and headed toward the kitchen. Callie would be nosy—she always was—and she'd want to know what was in that room.

Either he was going to have to get her drunk every night, because he never took advantage of a woman who had too much to drink, or he was going to have to let her go back to the inn or to the motel once the weekend people went back to the mainland.

She groaned as she sat down at the island.

"Not feeling so well this morning?" he asked.

"Why did you let me drink so much?" She took the mug of coffee he offered.

"I tried to stop you, but you told me you'd toss the bottle at me like you did the ring."

"Umph." She smacked her hand against her forehead. "You must hate me for losing that ring. It must have set you back a pretty penny."

"You'd vomit a little in your mouth if I told you what I paid for it."

"It was a gorgeous ring, and I'm sorry I lost it so

you couldn't return it. I should find a way to pay you back."

"You know what." He leaned against the counter, holding his mug and staring into her dark-chocolate eyes. "Us being able to apologize to each other and spend time together without killing each other is payback enough."

"You're a good man, Jag."

"Can I have that in writing?"

"Abso-fucking-lutely *not.*"

He leaned in and kissed her cheek. "I'm going to get the paper. I just have to go into the office for a few hours today. I thought maybe we could break out the Harley and take a ride."

"I think I'd like that," she said with a smile. "You're a dangerous man, Jag."

"Why? It's not me that will be between your legs. It's my bike."

"You are a pig." She slapped his shoulder.

He shrugged as he made his way to the front porch. He pulled open the door and bent over for the paper. When he lifted it from the ground, two envelopes spilled out onto the wood deck. One had his name on it. The other had Callie's.

Fuck.

He did a quick scan of the area before he pulled out his cell and found Jenna's contact information. She was probably still in the office. "Hey, Callie. Bring me a pair of gloves. They're under the sink."

"Okay," she called.

"What's up, Chief?" Jenna asked.

"I think I might have a situation at my place. I need you to head over with a couple of evidence bags."

"Please tell me we're not going to have to call the CSI team again."

"I can't make that promise," he said. "See you soon." He tucked his cell in his back pocket.

"What's going on?" Callie pressed a hand on his back. "Oh. What are those?"

He took the gloves. "We're about to find out." He glanced around one more time, making sure nothing looked out of the ordinary. And nothing did. Of course, his security system recorded all entrances and kept those recordings for forty-eight hours, so he should be able to see who dropped off this little gift.

"I don't like that people know I'm staying here," she said. "I mean, Bailey has a big freaking mouth. I can only imagine what she's telling people. I should have never met with her."

"No. I think you did the right thing. People are talking and speculating. I'm actually thinking you might want to call Jackie now and set something up. Do it live. Beat Bailey at her own game. We could do it together." Did all that just come out of his mouth? His mother was going to have his hide, and if he were a teenager, his father would take the car keys and ground his stupid ass.

But he was a grown man, and for the last year, he'd been hiding out on this island, isolating himself, living with ghosts, yearning for the living and wishing he could find a way to make up for the past.

Maybe this was it.

Carefully, he picked up both envelopes and brought them into the kitchen. "Does the handwriting look familiar?" He studied it for a moment. The letters were block style and bold. It reminded him of his own handwriting when he was trying to be as neat as possible.

"Yeah. Yours."

He chuckled. Taking a butter knife, he sliced open each of the casings. Three round pendants fell from both.

"Those look like they go to charm bracelets or something," he said.

There were two matching gold ones.

Two matching silver ones.

And two matching rose gold ones.

"Are those ravens etched into the charms?" Callie asked.

"Looks like it. Do they mean anything to you?" Using the knife, he pushed all six charms around on the table, lining them up in two rows, equal distance apart. "Other than the obvious creepiness of ravens to begin with, they could be considered trinkets, not charms."

A tap at the front door made them both jump.

She grabbed his biceps and gasped.

"It's just Jenna," he said, letting out a puff of air. "Do you mind putting on a pot of coffee?"

"I'll try not to blow anything up," she mumbled, still squeezing his forearms. "This isn't happening. He's not back. This is some asshole fucking with you. Or me. Or both of us. But it's not the Trinket Killer."

"I hope for both our sanity that you're right."

But something told him that his worst nightmare was about to come true.

Callie sprawled out her research across Jag's kitchen table. Twisting her hair, she pooled it in a messy bun on top of her head and shoved her glasses up on her nose.

The Trinket Killer changed from gold to silver at the sixth victim.

Stephanie was number twelve.

If he were following a pattern, he should have changed the color of the trinket. But her sister's death seemed less organized than all the rest. It just always felt different to her.

Maybe Stephanie wasn't supposed to be number twelve.

Callie attached the images of the raven pendants and sent them in an email to Kara. They might mean something to her.

The other issue had been the cooling-off period. The Trinket Killer had been a patient killer and his twelve murders spanned over five years.

But Stephanie happened two weeks after the last one and that didn't make sense.

Her editor's number flashed across her cell screen.

"Hi, Jennifer," she said. Jennifer Ruley was a hard-ass editor, but Callie loved her, even when she didn't agree with her suggestions.

"I've good news. The publisher likes the new title, and they want to go with that."

Callie let out a sigh of a relief. Jagar wouldn't be thrilled the book was still being published, but this might ease his frustration with her a little. "Thank you for pushing that for me."

"My pleasure, but they really want a chapter about Detective Bowie whether it's authorized or not," Jennifer said.

Callie took off her glasses and tossed them on a stack of papers. She and Jag had been getting along so well. This would completely destroy what little trust and understanding they'd regained with each other.

Maybe he would change his mind and give her an official statement. If not, at least she wouldn't have to tell him until after the book was turned in and she hightailed it out of Seattle. She never had any intention of staying here more than a month anyway.

"I'm working on it," Callie said. She clicked on the folder that had her notes for Jag's chapter. "I'll be able to shoot this all back to you in two weeks."

"Why can't all my authors be like you and turn things in on time or early," Jennifer said. "Let me know if you need anything."

"Will do."

As soon as she ended the call, another one came through.

Kara.

"Hey there," she said. "How's Oregon?"

"It was great until I opened your email a second ago," Kara said. "What the hell? I leave you alone for five minutes, and you've got a stalker already?"

Callie let out a nervous laugh. "Jag has me going through all the weirdos who send me stuff at the station while he's going through all the people who hate him, but it comes down to the one thing that ties us together."

"His dick?"

"Don't be gross," Callie said. "I've never understood why you didn't like him."

"I like him. He's a good guy. He's just not for you."

Kara was probably right about that, only her heart told her otherwise.

"But seriously," Kara said. "If you're thinking the Trinket Killer sent you those charms, I'd say you're wrong. First, they aren't the kind of trinkets he used in the past. Second, there is no dead body. And finally, why three? He's never done anything like that before. Aren't you always the one telling me that when a killer breaks a pattern, there's a reason. So, what's the reason?"

"That's what I need to find out."

"You know, Ivy's got a thing for ravens."

"I didn't know that," Callie said. When Callie had first met Kara, she'd been a grieving widow who wanted answers regarding her wife's murder. Their friendship had started off slow, and at first, Callie would get annoyed by Kara's constant inquiries. But as time went on, Kara became a source of great information. She had an eye for detail and was an excellent research assistant both when Callie had been a reporter and when she'd chosen to become a crime writer.

It had taken Kara a long time to get over her wife's death, so when she started dating Ivy a few months ago, Callie encouraged it, only she wished she'd gotten to know Ivy better.

But instead, she spent all her time, according to Kara, living in the past and being hung up on three things.

The Trinket Killer.

Her sister's murder.

And Jagar Bowie.

It was the latter that always pissed off Kara to the point that their friendship had become strained over the last few months. That was, in part, why she hadn't known Ivy well.

"Yeah, well, it's not my thing, and honestly, it's more of a writing thing as in Edgar Allen Poe."

"Ah. That makes sense," Callie said. Ivy dabbled in writing short mystery fiction, but she hadn't had anything published yet.

"Would you like me to have her take a look at them and see if the pendants mean anything to her?"

"Yes, but please don't tell her why. This is an active investigation, considering the note I got at the inn the other day."

"Do you want me to come to Seattle?" Kara asked.

"No. That's not necessary." Callie stiffened her spine. For the last year, she'd come to rely on Kara a little too much. It was time for Callie to take care of herself. "Give Ivy my best."

"Talk soon and call me if you need to."

Callie dropped her head and rolled her neck.

"Hey, babe," Jag said, practically sneaking up behind her.

She jumped, knocking over a couple of files. "Shit."

"Sorry." He bent over and picked up the stack

before resting his hands on her shoulders, giving them a good squeeze.

She moaned. "You were always so good at that."

"Have you gotten any better?"

"I haven't given a massage since you," she admitted. "What did your security cameras catch?"

"I forwarded a link to you. I want you to watch. It's dark, and I'm thinking it's a woman, but I can't tell."

"Okay. I'll look now but only if you promise you'll give me a better rubdown."

"Babe, really bad choice of words," he said as he pulled up a chair, keeping one arm looped around her body. "Open up the email. It's only about ten minutes long."

She pulled up her email and clicked on the link.

A grainy video filled the screen. A dark-blue or maybe green four-door sedan rolled to a stop at the top of the hill. She could only see half of it, and she couldn't tell if it was a Honda or maybe a Toyota. But it was definitely a foreign model. Someone wearing dark clothing slipped from the car and zigzagged through the trees in the yard.

Whoever it was, they wore a ski mask and dark

clothes with black sneakers and black gloves. She could tell they were black set against the stark white envelopes, which the person carefully tucked into the newspaper.

"What time is your newspaper dropped off?" she asked.

"Usually around five. But all this is time-stamped, so that happened at five eighteen."

"Huh. I was awake," she said.

"Pisses me off to admit this, but so was I, though I was in the shower."

"I was just lying in bed, watching the news, but I was up." She leaned in, trying to get a closer look. "Whoever that is knew where your cameras were because they made sure their face was never captured."

"I noticed that," he said. "Sort of tall for a woman, short for a man."

"Could be either," she said. "I remember when Stephanie started to really transition. I thought I would always see my brother Steve, but it was like one day he melted away and there was my sister Stephanie, but oddly, in the dark, other than she grew breasts and long hair, she looked the same. I told her that once, and she didn't like it."

"Because you told her she looked like a man, which is the one thing she was trying to get away from."

Callie smiled. It had been hard for Stephanie. Most people didn't understand, and she got bullied a lot as a teenager. Even as an adult, Stephanie struggled to fit in to society.

Jag always made her feel like she was a beautiful woman. He even went as far as to set her up on a date with his cousin, Zane's brother. It didn't work out, but that's when Callie really knew Jag had stolen her heart forever.

"Good point," Callie said. "I have no idea who that is."

"Neither do I, but I sent it to the lab. Maybe they can enhance it."

She leaned into him, resting her head on his shoulder. "Kara warned me what coming back might do."

"It's not the first time someone decided to remind me that the Trinket Killer is still out there. When I first took this job, someone thought it would be funny to leave twelve different trinkets on my porch with a big sign calling me a murderer."

"You didn't kill those women."

His strong hands came down on her shoulders. He spun her around. The chair screeched on the tile floor. "That's not what you told the world the day we broke up, or your last day reporting for Channel 5. And then you went and told everyone about your theory and how I blew you off."

"Well, you did."

"Actually, I didn't," he said. "Ajax Bond and I sat and discussed that theory one night for hours. The problem with it was the blood DNA."

"But now we know that Armstrong tampered with those samples and actually placed Adam's at the scene," she said.

"But we didn't know that until after your sister's death. And since Armstrong is dead, we haven't been able to figure out a motivation for why she did that," he said, holding her gaze. "Had it not been for that evidence, I would have considered your theory that we had the profile all wrong and Adam wasn't our killer."

"This is a big never-ending fucking loop that has driven me crazy for the last year. The publisher is mostly fine with the book the way it is, but it feels unfinished. I agree."

"Because he's still out there." Jag took her chin

with his thumb and forefinger. "But have you ever thought he might be done? That whatever triggered him, or whatever he wanted to accomplish, is over? I stayed in Seattle, and it's been hard to let this all go, but part of taking this job was doing exactly that." He leaned in and kissed her softly. "Finish the book and move on."

"Let me interview you. I need a chapter just about you. A personal anecdote of some kind. That's really all I have left to do."

"If I agree, do you think you'll be able to walk away from the Trinket Killer once and for all?"

She nodded.

"All right. I'll do it on one more condition."

"What's that?"

"I get to kill anything in the chapter I don't like."

"I can live with that," she said.

He glanced at his watch. "I've got to go to the station. I don't like leaving you alone."

"I was thinking I'd go into town and work at the library while you were at work." While she didn't like admitting feeling that spooked, she had no desire to be looking over her shoulder. At least at the library, she'd be in the same building as Jag, and she could sit in the corner with her back to the wall and a good view of everyone who came in.

The library was that small.

Besides, she could look up old newspaper articles that she might have missed referring to the Trinket Killer.

Or Jagar Bowie.

6

"Thanks, Jenna." Jag tossed his overnight bag in the back of his Jeep. Callie was going to be pissed for about five minutes. Mostly because he went into her room and snagged a few of her things for an overnight without telling her. She always hated when he did that.

He thought he was being romantic and spontaneous.

She said it bordered on controlling and manipulative.

And then she settled in and had a good time.

But if he was going to open up to her for this stupid book, it was going to be on his terms.

Not hers.

"Anytime, Chief," Jenna said, leaning against his

SUV with her arms folded across her chest. "I checked the ferry logs, and Bailey left the island with her team an hour after she met with Callie."

"And you're sure she hasn't come back?"

"I'm positive. She was too busy fucking her boss."

Jag arched a brow. "Which one?"

"From the reputation that woman has, I wouldn't be surprised if she's slept with all of them. But currently, she seems to be having quite the passionate affair with the news manager, Todd Geoff. They think they are being discreet, but you wouldn't believe how easy it was to find that out."

"How can you be sure she was with him this morning?"

"Because they were both in Crystal's Cake Bakery at about eight." Jenna waved her index finger in the air. "Todd licked icing off her finger. Crystal said it was the grossest thing she'd ever seen."

"I bet. How are Crystal and Albert?" Jag asked. It had been a while since he'd seen Detective Albert Morning or his lovely bride. Ever since he moved out to the island, he'd pushed his old life away, Albert included.

"They're good. Albert asked about you, especially how you're holding up since Callie blew back into town."

"I'll give him a call next week. Thanks again for everything. You know how to reach me."

Jenna tapped the hood of his Jeep. "Be safe, Chief." She strolled toward the parking lot and her patrol car.

He slipped behind the steering wheel and waited for Callie. It took her another ten minutes before she left the library and meandered down the walkway with her knapsack slung over her shoulder.

She had pulled her long blond hair into a high ponytail. A few strands lined her oval face. She waved, pushing her dark sunglasses up on her nose. "Where are we going?"

"Get in and get buckled."

"Oh, God," she mumbled as she pulled the strap across her chest. "What have you done?"

"What the hell does that mean?" He revved the engine before putting it into gear and pulling out onto the street. "Why would you think I've done anything?"

She laughed, glancing over her shoulder. "Because we're taking the Jeep, not the Harley, which means there are clothes in that bag, and I bet there's camping equipment in the back."

"There's always camping stuff in my SUV, you know that."

She tilted her head and glared. "I'm not going to go camping with you."

"If you want to interview me, then yes, you are; otherwise, I'm not doing it." He gunned the vehicle, heading toward Fort Casey. After Callie dumped him and his captain forced him to take a leave of absence, he spent a month camping at various campgrounds.

Fort Casey had always been his favorite.

Of course, it had also been one of Callie's favorite places when they'd been dating.

She kicked off her shoes and put her feet on his dashboard.

"Um. What are you doing?" He glanced in her direction. "You know I hate that."

"Payback is a bitch," she said, snapping her jaw and giving him a wickedly sarcastic smile.

"I guess I deserved that." He took off his shades and set them in the center console. The sun settled behind the mountains, and the fog rolled in, hugging the roads like a ghost floating through a cemetery, stretching his fingers, reaching out into the night for something to grab hold of.

By the time he pulled into the camping area, the

night sky had completely taken over. He went about putting up his roomy four-man tent with a space heater while she set out the fried chicken meal he'd picked up at Star Market on the picnic table. He rolled out both sleeping bags. A year ago, he would have turned them into a double bed, but now he contemplated putting up a drape, creating two rooms.

Fuck it.

If she wanted him to, he'd do it when they went to bed.

"So," he started as he stepped from the tent. "What kind of angle are you taking with this chapter dedicated to me? I mean, you spent a ton of time already discussing my mistakes."

"The publisher wants me to cover what your thoughts are on the case now. I hadn't planned on taking that approach, but I think it's a good one. That is if you were willing to talk to me."

"And what had you considered doing?" He straddled the bench and grabbed a piece of fried chicken. "If I chose to keep my lips sealed."

"Honestly?"

"Please," he said, licking his fingers.

"I didn't think you'd let me interview you. So I was going to do the old talk to all your friends and family. Ask them about how you were handling what happened. And if no one really talked, then I'd go with the ex-fiancée angle and what I thought of what transpired and make assumptions."

"Oh, that could seriously be a low blow." He bit into the cold chicken and closed his eyes. "Oh, my God, this is good." When he blinked them open, she'd cocked her head and glared at him. "What?"

"Do you really think I'd hit you below the belt?" she asked.

He nodded. "Based on the eight pages earlier in the book, yeah."

"Okay. I guess I deserved that," she said, waving a drumstick in his face. "But for the record, the publisher's notes have me toning it down and bringing it to about four pages, so you won't look like such a dick."

"Gee, thanks."

"You're welcome," she said with a slight laugh.

"But you were right. I fucked up big-time. I had no reason to arrest him until after the search warrant had been executed. I jumped the gun because I wanted so desperately to believe he was guilty."

"Wanted to believe? Are you saying you didn't?"

"I told you I spent a long time discussing your

theory with Ajax. I also discussed it with Albert Morning. Do you remember him?"

"Isn't he married to Crystal, the owner of that awesome cake bakery?"

"That's the one," Jag said. "Albert wondered if the FBI profile might be off, but we couldn't come up with one that fit either, especially since we never could agree on the killer's motivation."

"It would have been easier if it was sexually motivated," she said.

Oh boy. This was not going to go well; he could feel it. "Maybe, but we had straight, lesbian, bi, and a transgender. But often violent crime scenes point to sexual motivation."

"What?" She dropped her piece of chicken on the paper plate. "My sister's was pretty brutal. But I don't remember any of the other victims being beaten and stabbed more than three times."

"Renee had been beaten almost beyond recognition, and she'd been stabbed twenty-one times, much like Stephanie."

Callie gasped. Her chest rose up and down as she took a few harsh breaths. "Why the fuck didn't you tell me?"

"It took a while before we could lump Renee in with the Trinket Killer because of that discrepancy with the next couple of victims, but the Trinket Killer left me a little note letting me know Renee was his work."

"What kind of note?" she asked with narrowed eyes. "And when?"

"Right after you dubbed him the Trinket Killer, he sent me an envelope with a picture of Renee at the crime scene, alive. Told me to make sure he got credit for all his kills. Seemed he got off on the way you told his story."

She picked up her chicken and tossed it at him.

He ducked, but it still managed to hit him on his temple. "Hey."

"You should have told me."

"I couldn't. It was one of those things we kept from the public and the press. Technically, I shouldn't be telling you now. So I'd rather you didn't print it in your book."

"If I can't print it, why'd you tell me?"

He shrugged. He really didn't know why he decided to fill her in on some of the things he hadn't been able to in the past. Maybe it was because she wasn't a reporter and he wasn't working the case anymore.

Or perhaps it was because he wanted to put the past where it belonged, and it was high time he found a way to forgive her for breaking his heart.

"I wanted you to know."

"Doesn't make me feel any better." She took a napkin and dotted the corners of her eyes. "The detective that took over for you, in his statement after my sister's murder, he said he believed that she knew her attacker. Do you believe that?"

"I believe that of both Renee and Stephanie. Their deaths were so brutal, but the killer took the time to clean them up. Whereas the rest, the killer only positioned the bodies a certain way to present the trinket. He didn't seem to care about them. He cared about Stephanie and Renee. It's why I don't think we'll be hearing from the Trinket Killer again. Your sister and Renee are like bookends. I just don't know what the story is in between."

"Do you even care what that narrative is?" She bolted off the bench. "No. You don't because you've done nothing to find my sister's killer since you were forced off the case."

That wasn't true. Not even close, but he wasn't ready to show her exactly how much time and energy he'd spent searching for a ghost. He wasn't sure if it was because his ego couldn't handle the fact he'd found almost nothing.

Or he was still holding on to the notion that he'd tell her when he found something.

"You don't know what you're talking about," he said.

"Fuck off," she mumbled, storming off into the tent. She tossed out one of the sleeping bags and zipped up the flap. "You can sleep in the damn Jeep."

Callie lay on her back and stared at the ceiling of the tent. Her eyes burned, unable to release the tears that stung at the corners. Memories of Stephanie flashed through her mind. They had been close their entire lives, and she helped her sister navigate her transition and subsequent surgery into becoming the woman who had been trapped inside the male body she'd been born with.

A few days before Stephanie had been killed, she'd called Callie, all excited about a new girlfriend, but it was new and she wasn't ready to share. Callie suspected it was because Stephanie hadn't told her new friend she was a transgender woman. Even with having had the surgery, it often freaked people out, and many didn't understand.

Poor Stephanie had many friends who thought they were open-minded, but it turned out they weren't even close, leaving Stephanie with a wounded heart.

But on the night of her death, she'd left a frantic message, begging Callie to call her. However, Callie had been having a romantic evening with Jag who had popped the question. When the call came over that the Trinket Killer had struck again, they were in bed, celebrating.

The sound of metal ripping open caught her attention. "I told you to sleep in the Jeep."

"Yeah. Well, that's not going to happen." Jag stepped into the tent, tossing the sleeping bag onto the foam mattress. "There is a divider you can put up if you want, but the space heater is on my side, and that will keep the warmth mostly with me, and it's already dropped to about forty degrees outside. But that's your call." He shimmied out of his jeans before hiking up a pair of sweatpants and slipping into the sleeping bag. "And for the record, I've never stopped looking for your sister's killer. Never. But it's fucking damn hard when the trail is as cold as it is." He rolled, turning his back to her. "Good night."

"Have you uncovered anything? Because I have

come across some things when it comes to my sister, and I have some new theories."

He chuckled. "I'm sure you do."

"That doesn't answer my question."

"I have a new theory, but it doesn't fit the FBI profile, and when I've talked to Albert and Ajax, they've poked holes in it."

She reached out and rested her hand on his back. "Jag. Talk to me. Please. I'm sorry how I reacted."

He rolled, tucking his hands under his cheek. The light from the lantern lit up his dark eyes. "A lot of people don't understand that your sister was a lesbian. They think because she was born with male parts that as a woman she still liked women and that as a man she must have been straight." He let out a long breath. "Stephanie was a gay woman who just happened to be transgender. Renee was a gay woman. I think whoever killed them might have been their gay lovers."

"Wait. Are you suggesting that Renee was cheating on Kara?" She propped herself up on her elbow. "Kara always said they had such a great relationship, and just about everyone I talked to said they had the kind of marriage most of us dreamed of having."

"Well, as you know, Renee's hairdresser told the police that Renee was thinking of leaving Kara."

"That's why the cops thought Kara could have killed Renee, but she was cleared pretty quickly."

"After I was reinstated and I had some time to lick my wounds after we broke up, I went back to that theory, and I found something disturbing."

Callie found herself snuggling closer to Jag as he wrapped his arm around her waist.

Old habits died hard.

"What was that?"

"Renee did have an affair with a woman by the name of Alley Gilbert. It was a short fling, and Alley thought no one knew about it. She also didn't know Renee had been murdered since the affair happened right before she was deployed for six months, and when she came back, she reunited with her girlfriend and got married. It wasn't until you named the killer that she even knew, but she never said anything until I started poking around."

"So, it couldn't have been this Alley chick?"

"Nope."

"But if Renee cheated once, she could have cheated another time," Callie said. "As my sister always said, once a cheater, always a cheater."

"I don't know if I buy that, but in this case, if

the Trinket Killer is a woman and knew both Renee and your sister, then it's possible."

"Why didn't you tell me about her?"

"I didn't know until about six months ago, and we weren't talking right around that time." He scooted a little closer, pulling down the zipper of his sleeping bag.

"What are you doing?"

"It's cold."

She laughed. "The heater is on."

"We'll be warmer this way." He fiddled with the clasp of her bag, tugging it down slowly. He groaned. "Jesus. Aren't you freezing?"

"I am now," she said, moving as quickly as she could to connect the two sleeping bags so he'd stop staring at her in her bra and panties.

"I packed you a shirt and sweatpants."

"I left it in the back of the Jeep, and I wasn't in the mood to face you," she admitted.

"Here." He pulled his shirt over his head. "You can wear that; I'll keep the pants though."

"Deal." She quickly wiggled the cotton fabric over her body, enjoying the fresh pine scent that smelled exactly like she remembered. When they'd been a couple, she used to love to grab one of his shirts and sleep in it when he was working late or not going to be around that night. He had a thick outdoorsy scent that reminded her of being in the woods in the spring when all the trees were blooming.

"Come here," he whispered.

She rested her head on his chest and splayed her hand over his stomach. "Did Kara know her wife cheated on her?"

"I don't think so."

"Good. That would have broken her heart, and it's bad enough her wife was murdered." By the time Callie had met Kara, it had been more than a year since Renee had passed. While Kara was still bitter and angry, she was more interested and curious in the process of finding a serial killer.

And helping in any way she could.

It became her passion.

Until the Trinket Killer just stopped killing.

Of course, there had been Stephanie's murder, which changed things for Callie, turning her into a crazy woman, and Kara nearly walked out of her life.

"But if Kara had known or suspected? Well, you know where my mind goes," he said.

She lifted her head, pressing her chin on his shoulder. "But that doesn't make sense."

"I know. A few months ago, I tried to put Kara at all the crime scenes or connect her to them, but I got nothing. Plus, what would be the motive? Especially to kill your sister. So I then tried to trace it back to this Alley chick, and I thought I was getting somewhere, but she was deployed during three other murders, including Stephanie's." He rubbed his hand up and down her back in a tender, loving motion. Just like he'd done so many nights when they'd been together. "But my investigation has pretty much stalled out there."

"Thank you."

"For what?"

"For at least trying."

"Besides being the detective in charge when we realized we had a serial killer, I cared about Stephanie. She was my friend. She was going to be my sister-in-law. I loved her too, you know."

"I know." She kissed his chest. "Do you really think we could be looking for a woman?"

"Female serial killers are rare, but they exist."

"But do they kill that violently?" she asked.

"I've seen some pretty gruesome things in my day, and some of them have been achieved by girls."

She inhaled sharply, letting it out in a big puff.

He reached out and tucked a piece of hair behind her ear. He gazed into her eyes, holding her captive. A year ago, all her hopes and dreams came in the form of Jagar Bowie. He was the sun that warmed her skin and the air that filled her lungs.

But they were doomed from the beginning.

She knew it then, and she knew it now.

Yet, if he kissed her, she wouldn't stop him.

His warm hand slipped under her shirt. His fingers fiddled with the elastic on her thong.

Her breath came in short choppy pants as she continued to stare into his smoldering gaze. He'd been an intense and demanding lover, but she freely caved to whatever he wanted, because she craved exactly the same thing. Their lovemaking had often been rough and urgent. It was as if they could never quite get enough of each other.

Or they were terrified that it would all be over tomorrow.

Right now, lying in his arms, she just wanted to enjoy the moment.

"Do you remember the first night we camped here?" he asked.

She laughed. "You sent me a text daring me to meet you at the ferry dock. We'd only been out together once or twice."

He lifted his head and gently brushed his mouth over hers. "We had wild, crazy sex twice. I wouldn't call that having gone on a date. Our little camping trip would be what I consider that. It's where we really got to know one another as people, not adversaries."

She palmed his cheek. "Why'd you bring me here tonight?"

"To remember who we once were and to forgive all the crap." He curled his fingers around her wrist. "When you showed up at my apartment to tell me you were leaving Seattle and you planned on writing this book, we both ended up saying a lot of shitty things to each other. I honestly believed I'd never see you again. I thought my heart stopped at Ajax's send-off party. I wanted to hate you. I wanted to blame you for everything that happened, and I really tried to. I'd been holding on to it for so long that I believed the narrative I had created. However, the truth is you said some things that hit too close to home, and I didn't want to take a deep look at myself. Moving to Whidbey, and giving myself some space and time, forced me to do exactly that."

"I know what you mean. You were right about certain character flaws about me." She snuggled in closer, pushing her knee between his legs. "Can we just let all that go now and work together so I can get the book done and maybe give the cold case unit something to work with? My goal is still to find Stephanie's killer."

"I'm good with all of that as long as you don't let it consume you. I want you to promise me that you will write your next crime book and move about the country and live your life. Don't stay stuck."

"I promise." Lying to him came too easily. She'd never put finding Stephanie's killer on the back burner. It would always be the first thing on her mind and when any lead came her way, she'd drop whatever she was doing to pursue it.

She just needed a damn lead.

He threaded his fingers through her hair and kissed her hard. His tongue pushed through her lips and assaulted her mouth with passionate desperation. He rolled to his back, pulling her body over his.

They fit together like an old leather driving glove. A little tight to pull on, but once settled against the skin, it was as if it had never been removed.

She straddled his waist and rose up, lifting the shirt hem.

His fingers dug into her thighs, and his dark eyes widened with delight the second she tossed the piece of clothing to the side.

Immediately his hands reached up and unhooked the front clasp of her bra. He pressed his hot lips against the space between her breasts, his thumbs and index fingers pinching and twisting each nipple.

She cradled his head in her hands, guiding his mouth to one of her exposed tits, and stared at him while she slowly and deliberately rolled her hips.

He hissed. Grabbing her ass, he lifted her off him and flipped her onto her back with a thud.

"Umph."

"Sorry, but not really," he said with an amused smile. He jumped to his feet, kicking off his sweats.

"Then you won't be mad when I do this."

She knelt in front of him, slipping her fingers into the front of his underwear.

"I could never be mad when your hands are… oh, dear Lord," he said with a throaty groan.

Cupping him with one hand, she gently ran the other one up and down the length of him, his hard skin soft and supple. She watched in glorious wonderment as she stroked and massaged him. She'd had a couple of short-lived affairs in the last few months, but not only did they mean nothing, they weren't very satisfying.

A slow, warm shiver weaved up her body like an ocean lapping at the shore.

He pooled her hair on top of her head.

She glanced up at him and smiled just as she flicked her tongue out, rolling it over the tip.

"Oh fuck," he said, tossing his head back and holding her hair a little tighter. "Sweet Jesus, you're good at that."

"You said that our first night together." Closing her eyes, she took more into her mouth, concentrating on the groans and hissing noises coming from his as well as the way his hand tugged slightly at her hair. He never pushed or forced her. She always figured that was his way of keeping some kind of composure.

"And I wasn't lying. Best I've ever… oh, my motherfucking God." He tugged her head, pulling her off him, and dropped to his knees, shoving his tongue deep in her mouth, swirling around, finding every crevice. His hands fumbled with her thong as he pushed her to her back, pulling the flimsy undergarment to her ankles and tossing them across the tent. He rested her legs over his shoulders and licked his lips. "It's not completely shaved like it used to be, and let me tell you, I love it." He didn't waste any time diving between her legs.

A wave a dizziness filled her brain. She blinked. And blinked again, trying to make the tent stop spinning, but it didn't work.

She dropped her head back and tried to take in a deep breath, but with his hands on her breasts, and his tongue swirling over her hard nub, it became impossible.

He continued to tease her, bringing her body close to the edge, only to pull back and not let her go over. He'd been a master at bringing her to the kind of climax that went on for a good ten minutes. It was never just one orgasm. It was five or six, one right after the other, never giving her a rest in between. It built up deep in her gut, growing from a tropical storm into a category five hurricane that covered her entire body.

"Oh, dear, God," she said, stiffening her lower body and gritting her teeth. If she wasn't mistaken, he chuckled.

Which only made her stomach tighten more. Her toes curled, and she dug her heels into his back Her fingers dug into the scalp of his head as she tossed hers back and forth. "Why do you do this to me?"

He lifted his head, licking his lips, and smiled. "Because I can and because you love it."

"Oh, yes, I do."

He slipped two fingers inside, curling them upward, reaching the sweet spot while his tongue danced on her hard nub like a feather floating in the air. He nipped at it with his teeth, sending her over the edge for the first time.

"Yes," she whispered as the first wave made her tummy quiver.

"Do you want more?" he asked.

"Stop torturing me."

He chuckled. "Babe, you live for me to torture you." He sat between her legs, teasing and tasting, plucking and twisting until she called out his name over and over again.

"Please," she begged. Her body shook like a herd of elephants on the run from a group of hungry lions. Each orgasm more intense than the other and her mind, body, and soul braced for final impact.

"Gladly." He lifted her off the floor, turning her to all fours, spreading her legs, and easing inside.

She arched her back, leaning into him, raising

up on her knees, and reaching behind her so she could wrap her hands around his neck.

He grabbed ahold of her breasts, squeezing them tight as he drove himself deep inside her. She had to fall forward, pressing her hands against the ground just to remain upright.

"Jag," she whispered, her body betraying her as another climax tore through her muscles. It was so intense she shifted forward, stretching out on her stomach.

He rammed into her three times before arching his back and groaning. He held that position for a good minute before he slowly lowered himself to the side, pulling her to him and kissing her neck. "I've never had any control when I'm with you." He pulled the sleeping bag up over their bodies.

She let out a long sigh. "Jag?"

"What, babe?"

"You know I truly, honestly loved you, right?"

"I know," he said. "I loved... I still love you. I probably always will. I guess that's what they say about first loves."

She closed her eyes tight, squeezing out a couple of tears. "I still love you too. Only, we're not the same people we used to be."

"Thank God for that." He kissed her temple.

"Get some sleep. I'll answer all your questions for your book in the morning."

Callie let her body relax as she took in a few cleansing breaths. She wasn't even sure of what she wanted to ask anymore. All she knew was that as much as she loved him, he couldn't be in her life long term.

7

Jag blinked open his eyes and smiled. His heart swelled. It had been a long time since he woke with the woman he loved more than life itself in his arms. It felt surreal.

But he knew it wouldn't last because he knew she would never give up her search for her sister's killer. She would never be able to put anyone else before finding Stephanie's killer.

He could understand that, and he didn't blame her. He certainly wasn't mad at her for it. If it were one of his siblings, he'd never rest until he brought the murderer to justice.

Hell, he wasn't about to let it go until Stephanie and all the other victims had a voice, and that meant he had to find the Trinket Killer if it was the last thing he did.

He hugged Callie close, kissing her temple before slipping from the makeshift bed and hiking up his jeans and pulling a sweatshirt over his head. Last night had been about forgiveness. It had been their way of letting go of the past, showing each other that while they still loved and cared for one another, they were moving on.

It was a goodbye of sorts, and he could live with that.

He slipped from the tent and shivered. The weatherperson had mentioned that the temperatures would drop back to what would be considered normal for this time of year, but it still chilled his bones. He managed to start a fire and put on a pot of water to make instant coffee. It would taste like tar, but it would do the trick to wake up his brain.

And calm his libido.

Because last night couldn't happen again.

It would break his heart.

He flipped open the cooler and pulled out the eggs and sausage he'd packed and prepped them. It wasn't going to be a five-star breakfast, but it would get the job done. His cell vibrated.

Albert Morning's name flashed across the screen.

"Hey, man, what's up?" Jag asked.

"I've got some news for you. Where are you?"

"Camping at Fort Casey," Jag said.

Albert grunted. "That's interesting considering Callie's back in town."

"Don't go reading anything into it. She wanted to interview me for her book. I agreed, but I didn't want to do it in the office or at my home. I thought somewhere that put us both on common ground would be a good place to hash out something like that."

"You didn't need to give me a dissertation," Albert said. "Do you want to know what I've got?"

"I sure do."

"No prints on the trinkets left at your place, but we did find a local store that carries them, and it's the same one that carried all the other ones that the Trinket Killer left at all his crime scenes."

"Any idea when they were purchased?" Jag scratched the center of his chest, hoping it would help the heartburn that churned in his gut.

"The store owner said someone bought their entire stock about a month ago. Paid in cash. No receipt. Only remembers it was a woman, average height, thought maybe light-brown hair, but couldn't be sure because her hair was tucked up under a hat. The owner didn't think anything of it because the woman was on the phone talking to someone about how she found the perfect party favor," Albert said.

"And how many were in their entire stock?"

"Fifty at ten dollars apiece," Albert said. "That's a lot of cash to be carrying around these days."

"Sure is." Jag stood by the fire and stared out at the lighthouse. The salty air filled his nostrils, cooling his increasing anxiety. "When the Trinket Killer made his, or her, first purchase, it had been after Renee's murder, so they'd already had an attachment for the store. Did you ask if they had any of the original dolphin ones?"

"I did, and they haven't carried them since they found the Trinket Killer purchased them at their store."

"Thanks for letting me know."

"I sent all the information over to Detective Marlo at the cold case division. Let me know if you need anything else."

"Thanks, man, I appreciate it." Jag tapped the screen, ending the call, and shoved the cell in his back pocket.

A woman serial killer would shift the entire investigation.

Movement in the tent caught his attention. He glanced over his shoulder and smiled. "Good morning, babe."

Callie stepped from the tent wearing his long-sleeved shirt and sweatpants. She'd pulled her hair into a messy bun on top of her head.

His favorite look.

Especially after wild, passionate sex.

"This yo-yo weather is crazy." She rubbed her arms.

He pulled her in for a hug, pressing his lips on her cheek. "Do you have all your questions that you wanted to ask me with you?"

"Most of them are in my head, but my recorder is in the Jeep."

He dug into his pocket and pulled out the key, pressing the button. The Jeep beeped twice. "Let's get this party started," he said with a slightly sarcastic tone.

"I promise, I'll go easy on you."

"Right," he said with a chuckle, patting her behind as she jogged toward his SUV.

He went back to the open fire, his boiling water, and a couple of fried eggs and sausage links. He tossed them on a couple of tin plates and poured the thick coffee that smelled like burnt pavement. He picked at his food while she set up shop with a little more excitement than he'd like. He understood she wanted to humanize the detective who botched part of the case. If he were being honest with himself, her book was set up to show a series of events that led the police down a dangerous path.

A narrow road with tunnel vision.

One she as a reporter had traveled down as well.

She settled herself across from him and scarfed down a few bites of her food. "You always manage to make the best open-flame eggs."

He laughed. "You can keep stroking my ego all day long; I won't complain."

"You might when we're done with this interview." She pointed to the recorder. "Ready?"

"Go for it."

She hit the record button and announced the date and what the interview was for all professional-like.

Meanwhile, all he could think about was all the different ways he wanted to have sex with her again. It was a really nice distraction from what he was about to dive into.

"It's been a little over a year since the last time the Trinket Killer has struck. Looking back on the time you were the lead detective, or even the few cases you started off with as a beat cop early on, what do you wish you had done differently?"

"That's a loaded question." He waved his fork in the air. "I'm older, wiser, and have more information. Also, it's really hard to pinpoint a few things because it's like a game of dominos. Change one thing, and you change the entire trajectory, and then there could have been an entirely different set of problems. But if I had to pick something, it would have been the arrest."

"But we know now that Adam wasn't the Trinket Killer, so why would you want to do that differently?"

"For one, I fucked up, and that potentially cost your sister her life. Something that still gives me nightmares and I'm not sure I'll quite be able to forgive myself for it."

She reached across the table, but he jerked his hand away. This was a professional interview, and right now, he couldn't deal with feeling the tenderness lift from her skin to his, seeping into his heart, soothing his aching soul.

"But also, I can't help but wonder if I hadn't

jumped the gun, and the chaos that ensued because of it, if we wouldn't have realized that Armstrong had been tampering with evidence and planting it at crime scenes." He lifted his coffee and stared at the grinds floating at the top. He set the mug down, deciding the caffeine wasn't worth it. "And that's the other thing. I didn't see things that were right in front of my face that now seem so obvious, but when I go over all the evidence now, I still can't figure it out, and it's infuriating."

"I know the feeling," she said. "I recently sat down with the FBI profiler who originally created both the victimology report and the unsub description. He still believes both are spot-on. What are your thoughts?"

"I'm not a profiler, which is why we called in the FBI. They are experts in that kind of thing. That said, I do trust my instincts, and there were always a few things that didn't sit right with me and more so today."

"Do you care to share some of those theories?"

"Actually, I don't. At least not on the record. I did, however, share my thoughts with the cold crimes detectives handling the case."

She reached out and stopped the recording. "Okay. Off the record. This is where you were talking to me last night about the bookends and both Renee and Stephanie knowing the killer and it being a woman, not a man?"

He nodded. "I didn't mention this last night, but I think the victimology is linked to Renee and Stephanie. I just don't know how since they didn't know each other and have no real commonalities."

"Except Renee did have an affair and my sister had a secret girlfriend."

He let out a long breath. "Yeah. That could be the key right there." He pinched the bridge of his nose. "But that still doesn't explain why the Trinket Killer stopped killing."

She tapped the recorder. "Do you ever feel like he's watching you, waiting for the right moment to come out of murder retirement and kill again?"

"Every night before I close my eyes. And even more so now."

"Why?" she asked.

"Because you're here. I know that sounds crazy, but the second you walked back into my life, I half expected the killings to start again."

She nodded. "Let's talk about what happened after it was proven that Adam wasn't the Trinket Killer. How did your life change?"

He laughed, though it wasn't a haha funny

laugh. "I almost lost my job, for one. My fiancée dumped me. I realized I wasn't as good of a homicide detective as I thought I was. Basically, for about a month, my life spiraled out of control. Then my buddy Ajax Bond helped me pick up the pieces, and I landed this gig as chief of police in Langley."

"That's a big change," she said. "Are you satisfied and fulfilled in your new position?"

"I am," he said. "Maybe more so than when I was a detective. But to be totally transparent, I do spend time following up on what few leads come my way when it comes to the Trinket Killer. I feel like I owe it to all the victims, their families, and especially to my ex-fiancée."

She tilted her head and arched a brow. "Why?"

"You should know why."

"But I don't."

Now it was time to make it personal. He took her hand and kissed her palm. "The night I proposed. The night Stephanie died. I promised to love and protect you. I told you I'd always have your back. I also made a joke, though I was serious, that I would always investigate with you. I crossed a line when I told you certain things, and by doing so, I put you and your sister in the line of fire."

"We both crossed that line." She set her pen

down on top of her notebook and shut off the recorder. "I think I have more than enough. You'll get a copy before I send it to the publisher. I won't put anything in there that you don't want me to."

"I appreciate that."

"I want you to know something," she said.

"What's that?"

"I blame myself just as much, if not more, than I blame you for everything that happened."

"Babe, none of this is your fault."

"You warned me that giving the killer too much attention might escalate things."

"And I turned around and fed you information to give you the exclusive anyway. Besides, our killer didn't do anything for the attention of the masses. One thing I don't want in that book is that I think at some point, our killer started doing things to impress you or for you in some weird way, and that's why I've been so worried the killings might start again with you back in Seattle."

"I've never understood why you thought the killer had some sort of weird vibe for me."

He lowered his chin. "Seriously? The killer communicated to you, and we can't rule out that the killer isn't doing it again."

"Okay, first off. I was the most aggressive

reporter during that time, so it makes sense that the killer would reach out to me. And aren't you the one who told me the note and the trinkets are just whack jobs fucking with us?"

"That thing is off, right?"

She nodded.

"The raven trinkets were purchased at the same store as the dolphin ones, and they were bought in bulk a month ago."

"Oh fuck, that might not be good."

"Nope," he said. "It could be bad. Very bad."

Callie tossed her knapsack on her bed in the guest room. A couple of shiny objects bounced off the bed and rolled to a stop near her feet.

She bent over and picked up two raven trinkets.

One silver and one gold.

She dropped to her knees in search of the third one, but it was nowhere to be found. However, she did find a note with her name on it that read:

Callie: You disappoint me. I thought you'd have more strength. The game has begun.

Fuck.

Fuck.

Fuck.

She raced down the stairs, fumbling with her phone. She paced in Jag's kitchen with her cell pressed against her ear. "Come on, Kara, answer the damn phone." She peeked around the corner. Jag had slipped into his home office and shut the door. She'd give him a few more minutes before letting him know what she'd found.

"Hi, Callie girl," Kara finally said.

Callie plopped herself on the stool at the island and let out a long breath, fighting the tears stinging the corners of her eyes. "I need to tell you something."

"Why do you sound so ominous?"

"Because those raven trinkets I showed you? They were bought in bulk at the same store where all the dolphin ones were purchased."

"Oh no," Kara whispered. "Ivy and I were talking about the differences between a dolphin and a raven. A dolphin symbolizes harmony, resurrection, and protection. Ravens generally represent death, often predicting it. It's a really big jump for a killer to go from one concept to the other."

Callie had to agree, but psychopaths often made connections normal people couldn't possibly understand. "What about resurrection and death? They go hand in hand."

"I suppose. But one is sunshine and unicorns while the other is all Alfred Hitchcock," Kara said. "One is about balance, and the other really deals with the coming of something terrible."

One of the things Callie loved about working with Kara was that she constantly forced Callie to stretch her mind, examine every angle, even the ones that seemed so obscure that the ideas bordered on the ridiculous.

But Kara was often right on the money.

And something horrible was on the horizon.

Callie pinched the bridge of her nose. "What if we've had it all wrong from the beginning and the Trinket Killer is a woman?"

"Why would you say that?" Kara asked. "That's not anything we've ever really talked about before."

"I know you don't want to hear this, and I'm sorry to be the one to tell you, but Renee was having an affair."

A faint gasp echoed from the other side of the cell. "Why would you bring that up? Why would you tell me that? Are you trying to hurt me?"

"No. It's not like that. Whoever killed my sister and your wife knew them. That's a key connection," she said, taking a quick breath. "Did you get to see Renee's body?"

"I identified her, yes. Why?"

"Did you know all the details? How many times she was stabbed? What she looked like at the crime scene? Did the police show you any of that?" Callie asked, trying not to sound so desperate.

"The police tried to trip me up so that I'd admit to killing my wife or give them something they could arrest me for," Kara said with tinge of resentment hanging on her words. "Why are we talking about this?"

"I know the Trinket Killer is back, only I'm really thinking he's a she, and I believe both your wife and my sister knew the killer. But what's the connection? What's the common denominator?"

"Callie. Slow down and take a breath," Kara interjected. "Have you talked to Jag? What does he think about all this?"

"He hasn't said too much. He's eerily calm about the entire thing." One thing Callie had learned early on was not to always tell Kara what Jag's theories were. When she'd first met Kara, she and Jag clashed, which was understandable since Jag all but accused Kara of murder. It had taken a long time for the two of them to become friends.

"I'm not exactly sure what he thinks, except that I don't think he's ever really given up looking for the killer."

"Well, that's good. I'm glad someone is still looking, but you need to stop. Remember when you asked me to tell you if you crossed that line into the abyss? Callie girl, you're there."

"I'm not obsessed," Callie said. "I stepped foot in Seattle, and shit started happening, and today I found out that my sister's crime scene was identical to Renee's. Those two were different from all the rest. What does that tell you?"

"That the cops don't always tell the public and the press everything?" Kara said sarcastically.

"I can't believe you of all people are taking this piece of information so lightly," Callie said softly.

"I'm not. I find it disturbing, and it hurts my heart. But I lived in the past for a good five years. I'm not doing it anymore. I can't. But I swore to you I'd help you finish this book, so if you want me to come back, I will. All you have to do is ask."

Callie dropped her head to her forearm. No way would she ask Kara to come back. They'd been through a lot over the last couple of years, but it had become painfully aware to Callie that she'd been holding Kara back. That Kara had been trying to move on with her life, but Callie wanted to hold on to the pain and suffering a little while longer.

"No. I want you and Ivy to chase your hopes and dreams. I just wanted to keep you informed of what was going on here and ask about the ravens." Callie slumped her shoulders. For the longest time, Jag told her that Kara had formed an unhealthy attachment to her. That Callie had let Kara get too close, something a reporter should never do with a family member of a victim.

Maybe he'd been right back then, but now it was Callie who was holding on to Kara for dear life. It was as if letting go of Kara meant Callie had given up on finding her sister's killer.

"Come to San Francisco, Callie. You got the interview. You can finish the book anywhere. That place is no good for either of us."

When Callie did leave Seattle for good, it wouldn't be with Kara and Ivy. No. Callie needed to learn to rely only on herself. Her entire life, there had always been someone else there to hold her up.

First her parents.

Then her sister.

Jag.

And finally Kara.

Callie had to figure out what it looked like to be an independent soul.

"I can't. I'm sorry. I have to see this through."

"You know how to reach me," Kara said before the line went dead.

When Callie had left Seattle with Kara a year ago, the idea had been to write the book as a way to put the past where it belonged. She dove so deep into writing she hadn't realized her friend, and assistant, had started to live again, while Callie barely existed in the past.

She had to come to terms with the fact that Kara would be okay with not knowing. That, as she said, she'd done everything she could humanly possibly do, she needed to do what Renee would want.

Stephanie would want Callie to nail the bastard.

Sucking in a deep breath, she stood and smoothed down the front of her jeans. She reached up and pulled out her ponytail, shaking out her long blond hair. That was another thing that always bothered her. All the women had long blond hair.

Just like her.

And Jag always thought that the killer was trying to impress her or something.

She tiptoed around the corner. Damn door was closed.

Fuck it.

Grabbing the doorknob, she twisted it as quietly as she could, pushing the door into the room.

Jag rested his ass against a gray desk with his legs stretched out about a foot and his arms folded over his chest. He stared at a wall filled with images of dead girls.

The Trinket Killer crime scenes.

"What the fuck is this?" She shoved open the door. It hit the other wall with a thud and slammed back into her shoulder. She just shrugged it off as she moved to the other side of the desk.

"Callie." He stepped in front of her, grabbing her forearms. "You can't be in here."

"Like hell I can't." She wiggled her arms free. "This isn't a police precinct, so if those are official files, you shouldn't have them."

"You know how this works. I'm a cop who worked most of these cases from the beginning. I can have access how I want."

She ignored his words and focused on the images of her sister. She'd been there that night, and Jag had brought her to her sister's body. He'd held her while she cried. He stood there while she blamed him and then drove her home and held her some more.

Two days later, she humiliated him in front of the entire world because while he'd done all that, he'd still lied to her as he'd always done.

Story of their entire relationship.

An image of her sister's body was pinned next to an image of another woman, but Callie couldn't make out who it was.

"Is that Renee?" she asked.

"Yes," Jag said, clearing his throat. "Other than the beating her face took, the scene is identical to your sister's."

She raised her hand and waved it over all the images of all the other girls, noting the trinket in each hand. "Six gold dolphins and six silver dolphins. And there was an even amount of both purchased," she said mostly to herself.

"Even amount of raven trinkets purchased as well, but this time we've added rose gold."

"Obsessive-compulsive disorder."

"We established the unsub suffered from that."

She nodded. "This one has a thing for numbers. I'm thinking six is important. So is three, which goes into six, twice."

"It also could be twelve, because he stopped killing at twelve."

"Exactly," she said. She reached into her pocket and pulled out the two raven trinkets. "These were on my bed."

"You've got to be fucking kidding me," Jag said.

"I wish I were. I can't find the other one, and frankly, I don't think he, or she, left that one behind. What do you think that means?"

"That our Trinket Killer has already started another cycle of killing," Jag said. "We just don't have a body yet."

8

The only time Jag went to the mainland these days was for mandatory work meetings or when his family made him. He stood on the bow of the ferry and stared at the Seattle skyline. He used to love living in the city. All the people and the fast pace of city life.

He didn't miss it one single bit.

The closer the ferry dock came into sight, the faster his heart beat.

If his theory was correct, the Trinket Killer hadn't started with Renee.

But who?

And where?

And how they hell did they miss it?

He made his way down from the observation

deck to where he'd parked his Harley. Flipping up the kickstand, he revved the engine, following the line of cars off the ferry and onto the main road. He headed toward downtown and his old precinct. He hadn't set foot in that building in almost a year. When he'd walked out, he didn't think he had a career left. Forced into a two-month leave, he had a lot of time to think about his life and what he really wanted to do, and being a cop was all he'd ever known.

Thank God for Ajax.

Pulling into the parking lot of the 87th Precinct of the Seattle Police Department, he reminded himself that when he took the job, he'd made a promise to Stephanie while visiting her grave that he'd follow every lead.

Only, he hadn't had a lead in months.

And now he had more than he knew what to do with, and none of them made any sense.

He pushed open the door, and his ears were assaulted with confrontational communication at its best. Nothing like his nice little quiet station sitting next to the library in city hall. He nodded to the desk sergeant who buzzed him past the front desk.

"Morning's waiting for you in the conference

room," the sergeant said. "Do you remember where it is? Or should I get you an escort?"

"I'm sure I can find it." He stuffed his hands in his pockets. He noticed a lot of familiar faces and a few new ones as well. A lot could change in a year.

And a lot stayed the same.

He tapped his knuckles on the glass door.

Albert waved him in. "How's it going?"

"I've been worse."

"You've looked better," Albert said, giving him his best bro cop hug. "Thanks for coming to me."

"I just appreciate you hearing me out," Jag said. "I was hoping Jack Marlo would be here by now."

"He just went to the head," Albert said. "There's fresh coffee if you want it."

"Don't mind if I do." Jag poured himself some swill and made himself comfortable at the far end of the table. He flipped through some active homicide files that Albert had pulled for him, but nothing was remotely like the Trinket Killer.

The sound of boots scuffing down the hallway caught his attention. Jack Marlo entered the conference room. "Hey, Jag. Good to see you."

"You as well." Jag rose and shook Marlo's hand. "Were you able to find anything?"

"Not a single cold case in Seattle that fits the

Trinket Killer's patterns," Marlo said. "I widened the search and went to other offices in the state with similar parameters and got a few hits. I don't think they match. At least not with what we know about our killer."

Albert leaned against the table. "Yeah, but we've been banking on our killer being a man. The profile changes when we make it a woman."

"And we think she knew at least two of the victims intimately," Jag added. "Both of those victims had secret relationships. Callie is digging into the other victims' past love lives."

"But they weren't all gay," Marlo said.

"It's an angle, and with these new trinkets showing up at my doorstep, I need to check everything no matter how absurd." Jag tossed three coins he managed to pick up at the store so the rest could be logged into evidence. "So, my theory is we're about to hit round three of the Trinket Killer's cycle. What I need to find is round one."

"I pulled up every cold case that I could find," Marlo said.

"Yeah, but maybe we think we solved it." Albert held up his index finger. "I pulled this file this morning. I made the arrest. It was rock solid, but I've always wondered if maybe we made a mistake." Albert tossed another file on the table. "Hendrix was also found guilty of murdering his neighbor. The DNA on that nailed his ass. He even copped to it, but to this day, he swears didn't kill the other girls."

"When was this?" Jag asked.

"My first year as a beat cop. I chased him in a stolen vehicle. After the arrest, we found a couple of mood rings, and that's what this killer would leave at the scene," Albert said.

"How many kills?"

"Three in one year. All white girls between eighteen and twenty, and they all went to the same college and lived in the same dorm." Albert stood behind Jag and tapped one of the reports in the folder. "The man I arrested was the janitor at the school. It was believed the girls, all cheerleaders, teased him or emasculated him, and he got his revenge."

Jag remembered that case. It had an entire college community on edge for a year. "Were the girls stabbed?"

"The first one was hit in the head a few times," Albert said. "The other two were stabbed. There should be pictures in there. First victim was found on the school grounds. The other two were in parks."

"Like all of mine." Jag flipped through another page and tapped a pen against his temple. He pulled out all the images of the dead bodies. Each one had a mood ring placed on their left ring finger.

The marriage finger.

Interesting.

Especially when the man sitting in prison for the crimes was an older man.

"Why did he kill his neighbor?" Marlo asked.

"She rejected him. And she does look a lot like those girls, which is why we were able to make the stretch," Albert said. "But to this day, he swears he was wrongfully incarcerated for three murders."

"Do you believe him?" Jag asked.

"I didn't at the time," Albert said. "Because at the third crime scene, which was the neighbor's, the victim was clutching a mood ring. And let's remember, I wasn't a detective back then, so it was not my case. But when you asked to see all this, I started examining all the evidence again, and it turns out Armstrong logged in the mood ring for that crime scene."

"Fuck," Jag mumbled. "Armstrong mishandled a lot of my evidence and DNA."

"And then killed herself," Marlo added, shaking his head. "She handled a lot of evidence. I wonder how many she tampered with and why."

"We might never know the answer to the latter question," Albert said. "But this house is pulling all the cases with Armstrong's name on it. Now what's really interesting about what I've dug up so far, is that procedure was followed to the letter on every case, except the Trinket Killer and the ones we just mentioned."

Jag peered over the file. "Are you saying you think Armstrong is connected to the Trinket Killer?"

Albert nodded. "I'm pulling the autopsy report on Armstrong as well. I'll have everything sent to your office."

"Send it to me too," Marlo said.

Jag slammed the file shut. "Why do I get the feeling this fucking killer has been playing me for a long time?"

Callie stood at the end of the dock and watched a sailboat tilt over as the winds grabbed ahold of the jib. She covered her forehead with her hand, shielding the sunrays peeking through the fog floating above the sound.

The floorboard rattled.

She glanced over her shoulder.

"Ziggy," she said with a smile before practically taking off in a full sprint. She hugged Ziggy tight for a good three minutes.

"I can't believe you're here," Ziggy said.

"Me neither." Callie smacked her lips against Ziggy's cheek. "You are a sight for sore eyes."

"Aren't you supposed to be saying that about my brother?" Ziggy tilted her head and batted her thick eyelashes. "He's been a miserable prick since you left."

"He doesn't seem like it to me." Callie looped her hand through Ziggy's arm and led her down to the beach.

It was only about sixty degrees, but the sun warmed Callie's face, and the salty breeze filled her heart with a sense of calmness she hadn't felt in a long time. She knew the second she got off this beach and met with Jackie for this stupid interview about her book, which her publisher blindsided her with by putting the pre-order up, her mood would surely sour.

While she was happy they agreed on the new

title, and the cover was tasteful, she wasn't prepared for how real having it up for sale would make it.

She worried how Jag would take the news, especially when he saw his name right there in the product description.

"We all miss Jag on the mainland," Ziggy said. "But being out here, on this island, has done him a world of good."

"I noticed."

A few toddlers raced by chasing a puppy, their mother only a few steps behind. Callie used to daydream about the day she and Jag might get married and have a little brood of their own. They'd even started talking about that prospect, someday in the future.

She pressed her hand across her stomach. If he'd known she was pregnant when she left Seattle, he'd hate her, but it didn't matter. She miscarried less than a month after she'd left.

But the burning question had always been, would she have told him had she been able to carry the child to term?

Today, she'd like to think she would have told him long before the baby was born. But part of her wonders if she would have used it to stay away from Seattle altogether. The reality was, the only reason she came back had been for the interview. The publisher all but demanded it. And she knew it was best for the book. The more she thought about it, the more it simmered in her brain, the more she wanted to spend time in Seattle.

And time with Jag.

Something Kara warned her would be a bad idea. Something about history repeating itself.

"You being back in his life would be even better." Ziggy squeezed her hand. "He's really missed you."

Their families hadn't known about their relationship for very long, but Ziggy had been one of the first, and since she worked with her at the station, they became fast friends.

Best friends.

"I've missed him too, and while we've been able to heal old wounds, I don't think we would ever be able to be together again long term."

"Oh, so does that mean something kinky happened since you've been back? I know you're staying with him, and I heard through the family grapevine he went camping last night at Fort Casey."

Callie shook her head and let out a short laugh. "Nothing is sacred or private in your family."

"Hey, it was only a guess, but thanks for confirming it for me."

"You tricked me." Callie hip checked Ziggy.

"You would have told me anyway."

"True." If Callie told Kara, she'd get a lecture. Now all Callie had to do was brace herself for Ziggy and the rest of his siblings to push back hard for them to get back together.

It wouldn't happen.

It couldn't.

They were oil and water.

Ziggy paused and turned toward the sound. "Jag told me you plan on leaving in a couple of weeks."

"As soon as his chapter is done. He gave me an interview. Now all I have to do is write it and get him to approve it."

"Don't leave again." Ziggy turned. "He loves you, and I know you love him."

"Sometimes love isn't enough."

"It's always enough," Ziggy said.

Callie took her hands. "Your brother and I spent a year using and lying to each other all while falling madly in love. That has Greek tragedy written all over it. We're lucky one of us isn't dead."

"That's a cop-out. Do you want to know what I think?"

"Does it matter? Because I think you're going to tell me anyway." Callie turned and headed back toward the dock and the best fried clam roll on the West Coast.

"The two of you got together during a high-profile case where he couldn't give you, the press, the information you wanted, and you had to sneak around to get it. That made you adversaries."

"Why don't you tell me something I don't know," Callie said. There were times it took Ziggy way too long to get to a point. Normally, it was an endearing quality but not this afternoon.

"The two of you always supported each other. You bent over backwards not to step on each other's toes. And damn it, Callie, you love my stupid brother, and don't tell me you don't."

"Okay, I won't. But that's not the point. Our ship has sailed." The wind kicked up as she hiked the steps. She'd put in their order for the clam rolls when she'd gotten there, and they should be ready by now.

Along with hot cider.

Life didn't get any better than that.

Unless she was eating half-naked in bed with Jag.

"I disagree. I just think your sails are all tangled up and just need some straightening out. I wish you would stay a few months and give him a shot. He's a changed man. He's lost that chip on his shoulder, and he's mellowed a lot. He's certainly not half as cocky as he used to be. I really think losing you fundamentally changed him and on some levels for the best. But he's a broken man without you."

"I think he's a better man since I left." Callie approached the take-out window. "I have an order for Dixon."

The girl in the seaside restaurant handed Callie a big bag along with a credit card slip to sign. Callie tucked a five-dollar bill into the tip jar. She found a picnic table and pulled out what smelled like a little piece of salty heaven.

"That's bullshit. And I know it because I've been here for the last year. You haven't." Ziggy lifted her roll into the air and took a huge bite before her eyes rolled to the back of her head. "Damn. These are the freaking best."

"Better than even in Boston," Callie said.

"I'll take your word for it." Ziggy lifted a clam strip that had fallen from her sandwich and plopped it into her mouth. "But in all seriousness. I know he was really glad to see you."

"Yeah. Did he say that? Because when he first saw me, he couldn't get away from me fast enough."

"Because his heart is still raw."

"Not raw enough. He took Bailey out on a date."

Ziggy burst out laughing. "He was trying to replace you, only that chick is a bitch. He hasn't dated anyone since."

"I'm sure he's had a booty call or two."

Ziggy arched a brow as she wiped her fingers with a napkin. "He'll never get over you, and I can see it in your eyes. You're never getting over him, so just give up, cave to your desires, and get back together with my brother." She pointed toward the parking lot. "Looks like Jackie and her cameraman are here. I'll see you back at Jag's place."

"What?"

"He didn't tell you? I'm spending the night on the island. He said I could have the guest room since you're staying with him."

Callie narrowed her eyes. "He didn't say that."

"You know, my brother might not be as arrogant as he used to be when it comes to work, but he's still a cocky son of a bitch when it comes to you, so yeah, that's exactly what he said. See you in a bit." With that, Ziggy stood and practically skipped down the dock toward the parking lot.

Wonderful.

Jackie Cash smiled and waved as she sashayed her way down the wood planks with her cameraman one step behind. Her wavy brown hair bounced like a shampoo commercial against her shoulders. She had to be a good five foot eleven in flat shoes. She had a natural beauty and carried herself with an air of confidence that couldn't be mistaken for ego.

Something Callie had to admit she was a little bit jealous of.

"Callie Dixon," Jackie said. "It's good to see you."

"It's good to see you too." Callie leaned in and kissed her cheek before easing over to the bench that overlooked the beach. "I appreciate you coming out here to do this."

"Never in a million years did I think you would ever suggest I interview you."

"You should know that Bailey is going to run a piece about me tonight as well. I spoke to her, but it was off the record, and nothing like what I'm willing to tell you."

"She called me to tell me she had a piece about you." Jackie went about hooking up a mic to Callie's jacket. It felt strange to be on the other side of an interview. "I wouldn't be surprised if she took a negative approach."

"I know exactly the approach she's taking, and it's to make me look bad. She's more concerned that I'm going to ask for my job back."

"Are you?" Jackie asked. She took a step back and glanced down at her own microphone, making a minor adjustment.

"I have no desire to go back to that life."

"Too bad. You always kept me on my toes," Jackie said. "Anyway, basically I've been doing a series on unsolved crime in Seattle, so it's perfect timing. I want to focus on why you felt the need to write the book. I just want the personal angle. You got the questions I sent over, correct?"

"I did."

"Was there anything you want me to stay clear of?"

"Yeah," Callie said. "My personal relationship with Jagar Bowie."

"That's too bad. Everyone at the station wants to know if the two of you are back together or not."

"Off the record. We're not. We're just friends,

but on camera, if you ask me one question about our relationship, past or present, I'll pull the plug."

"I'll keep it to the book and the murders, period," Jackie said.

"Thanks." Callie stiffened her spine and pulled her hair back into a ponytail so the wind didn't take it and whip it in front of her face.

Here went nothing.

9

"Oh, for fuck's sake, stop acting like you're so pissed off at me." Jag pulled back the comforter on his full-size bed. He used to have a king in his apartment in Seattle, but living alone, with no girlfriend and no desire to have a warm body spend the night, what did he need a huge bed for?

Besides, while the master suite was massive with an extended sitting room and deck, the actual bedroom part was pretty cramped, and anything bigger than a queen wouldn't allow for even a nightstand on both sides.

"I am angry. You assumed, for the second time in two days, that I would be okay sleeping with you."

"That's not true." He stood at the foot of the bed with his hands on his hips, wearing only his sweatpants, while she wore only his undershirt and maybe a tiny thong underneath, but he couldn't tell. "When we went camping, I had the room divider and two separate sleeping bags."

"That you zipped together." She held up her hand. "And are you going to deny you told Ziggy that I wouldn't mind sharing your bed?"

He chuckled. "Well, no. But that was me telling my sister what she wanted to hear. Seriously, I have no problem sleeping on the sofa in the sitting room. Or if that's too close, I'll go to the couch in the family room."

"You'd really do that?"

"Go look in the other room." He stepped to the side so she could get a good look at the pullout that he hadn't made yet, but he'd put out all the necessary bedding.

"Oh. I see."

"So I'll sleep there. If you want. But I don't want to. I'd much rather sleep with you." He'd lost his mind.

And his heart.

He knew he'd never get either of them back, so he figured he might as well enjoy her while he could. Soon enough, she'd be walking out of his life again, and there wasn't a damn fucking thing he could do about it.

At least this time they'd be able to leave on good terms.

That might make it easier for him to pick up the pieces and fake a life.

"That is about the most passive-aggressive thing you've ever done," she said with a laugh as she climbed between the sheets. "I'm not going to kick you out of your own bed."

"So you're going to share it with me?"

"What the hell does it look like I'm doing?" she asked. "Now kindly tell me what you thought of the interview with Jackie and of Bailey's stupid piece on us."

Normally, he'd shed the sweats, but that would really be presumptuous, and he wasn't about to assume that just because she was willing to rest her head next to him that she wanted sex. If that were the case, she'd have to initiate it.

And even then, maybe he should turn her down.

Like that might be possible.

He sat on the edge of the bed, contemplating where he might actually sleep.

"Let's start with Bailey." He rubbed his temples. "It wasn't as bad as I thought it would be."

"She all but called you incompetent."

He chuckled. "She said that about the entire Seattle Police Department. But she had a quote taken directly from the chapter on the night we found your sister. It was as if she was reading from it. She said, '*The hush that had come over the city of Seattle when it came to light that Adam Wanton had been killed before Stephanie Dixon and that there was no way in hell he could have been the Trinket Killer was deafening.*' After I saw the piece, I had to go get the manuscript and look it up. It was almost word for word. How'd she get that? Because you told me that only a few people had gotten that draft."

"Actually, only five people had that copy. You, me, Kara, my editor, and my agent. But that's a pretty generic description."

"Come on. Are you really going to brush that under the rug?" He glanced over his shoulder. "So how'd she get a direct quote?"

Callie propped up the pillow and leaned against the headboard. "I have no idea, and before you keep pushing, I concede it sounded way too close to my words for it to be a coincidence."

"Babe, I looked it up. It was word for word." He arched a brow.

"Shit," she mumbled. "Any chance she could have seen your copy? I mean, you did fuck her."

"Jesus Christ, Callie. First off, I was so trashed I couldn't perform, so the fucking never actually happened. And second, it happened two months after you left. I was angry and lonely, and you probably hadn't even written a single damn word yet."

She covered her mouth and made a weird noise that reminded him of a combination between gagging and giggling.

It wasn't a pretty noise.

"I'm glad you find my failed manhood amusing."

"It's not that." She reached out and rubbed his shoulder with her deft fingers. "It's the way she tried to pretend you had a relationship and tried to use it to bond with me because she believes I think you're a total asshole."

"Back then you did too."

"But I don't now," she said. "I'm sorry I said that. I have to admit, I was jealous that you'd even think to be with her."

"I wasn't thinking, that's for damn sure. I've never been so disgusted with myself, and I've never been so happy to not be able to get it up. Thank God that was the only time that's ever happened."

"Maybe it wasn't all the drink and it was the woman?"

He twisted his body and stretched out his legs, leaning back on the headboard. "I like the way you think."

"Now that we've got my jealous rampage out of the way. How the hell did she get ahold of a copy of my manuscript? I know my editor wouldn't give her that quote. Not without running it by me first."

"Would Kara?" Jag hated asking that question. Kara had been a good friend to Callie, especially when Jag had been a jerk. But Kara had her own set of issues, and there were times Jag questioned Kara's motives. At one point, he wondered if Kara wasn't in love with Callie, but he knew now that he'd been jealous for no reason. "And I don't mean on purpose. I'm just asking if she'd give someone a quote without thinking."

"No. Not without asking me first." Callie dropped her head on his shoulder. "I did have a copy of the manuscript on the table when she got there. It's possible she saw something before I put it away."

"For now, we'll go with that, but I want you to

change your passwords and have a conversation with everyone who was given a copy."

"I can do that," she said. "But what about Bailey?"

"I'll handle her."

Callie poked the center of his chest. "I don't like the sound of that."

He grabbed her wrist and kissed the center of her palm. "Bailey was more embarrassed about my lack of performance than I was. As a matter of fact, she took it so personally that she's lied about it ever since."

"That's kind of pathetic on her part," Callie said. "But do you mind if we stop talking about her now? I'm actually really curious on what you thought about the interview with Jackie."

He raised his arm, wrapping it around her body and pulling her close.

So much for waiting for her to make the first move.

Well, she did touch him first.

"You were amazing."

"I was so pissed when she went off-script and asked about you and me. She promised she wouldn't. She swore she'd keep it strictly to the book," Callie said.

Jag had been just as shocked. He'd thought Jackie was more of a classy reporter than that, but since there was no news to report when it came to the Trinket Killer, why not go for the sensationalism and dirt. "She did handle the book stuff really well and got to the heart of the investigation. I particularly liked how she brought up Armstrong and how she's still such a big question mark in the case. We still have no idea why she planted DNA or mixed it all up. I know the department has been looking closely at all her work, and the Trinket Killer seems to be the only case she fucked up."

"Have you read her autopsy?" Callie asked.

"I have, and no, I'm not going to show it to you."

She glanced up at him. "Do you believe she killed herself?"

"The evidence is pretty damning for that conclusion." He pressed his fingers against Callie's lips when she opened her mouth. "I've thought about the idea the killer could have murdered her and set it up to look like a suicide. But I can't answer the question as to why Armstrong would help the Trinket Killer."

"Did you ever think that maybe Armstrong was the killer?" Callie asked.

"That's an interesting theory, and now that we think the killer could have been a woman, it's one that I've asked the cold case detective to look into, but my gut instinct says no." That said, he knew there was a connection between Armstrong and the killer.

He just didn't know what it was.

He reached for his iPad and pulled up his file on the subject. "I've done a lot of thinking over the last year about Armstrong. When we believed without a doubt that the Trinket Killer was a man, I wondered if Armstrong could have been his lover, and that's possible. But she's also bisexual."

"So she could have had an affair with the killer regardless of gender," Callie said. "But she didn't start doing it until the sixth victim."

"And that's what is fascinating to me." He handed her his iPad. "I just made this note today, but that's when the color of the trinket changed from gold to silver."

Callie sat up taller and scrolled through his detailed notes he'd been making for the last year. Every little thing he'd ever thought of. It was more of a flow of consciousness than anything else, so some things he'd already proven incorrect. But sometimes, going back and examining the way his mind pieced together the information as it was presented gave him insight.

Or it just made him crazy.

"And you really think the killings started before Renee?"

"If the three ravens are a precursor of what is to come, then there had to be a single trinket to start."

She handed him his iPad. "But the one you showed me didn't have six murders."

"Because they caught who they thought was the killer. I suspect if Adam hadn't been released, our killer would have stopped. We gave him or her permission to finish his cycle when Adam was proven not to be the murderer and was released."

"And Armstrong helped prove that right before she committed suicide," Callie said.

He pressed his lips against her forehead, sliding down onto the mattress. In the last couple of days, they'd uncovered more information than he'd been able to in an entire year. "We make a good team," he whispered. "That is when I'm not being an arrogant detective who thinks he knows everything and—"

"I'm not out for ratings, doing whatever it takes, including snooping in police files."

"We both made a lot of mistakes. We've both changed. Why aren't you willing to give us another chance?"

"There are a lot of reasons. One of which is I'm not willing to live in Seattle. Hell, I won't be staying in Washington State, and this is your home. It's where your family is, and I know you're never leaving."

He couldn't imagine leaving the Seattle area. Whidbey Island was about as far away from his siblings and his parents as he could stand to be. However, he watched Ajax leave the police force, a career he loved, for a woman he couldn't live without. Sure, they could have done the long-distance thing with Lorre's career, but Ajax wanted to be by her side.

He didn't want anyone else protecting her on a daily basis.

"I'd consider it for you," Jag said.

She kissed his chest. Her hot breath tickled his skin, sending goosebumps rippling across his body. "You'd be so unhappy anywhere else."

"I'm unhappy here without you." He rolled to his side, holding her close, looking deep into her dark-almond eyes. "Sure, I've survived. I'm going about my daily life. I put a smile on. I laugh. It's not the worst life, but it's not my best. That was always with you."

"Jag, please don't do this. I will always love you, and I know that will never change. But I'm not staying, and I won't have you leaving your family or your career to come with me when I don't even know what's next; only, I suspect whatever it is, it will happen in New York."

He jerked his head back. "You want to live on the East Coast?"

"It's the mecca of the publishing business. It's where my editor and agent are, and this book is getting the attention of some true crime television shows."

"And that's what you really want?"

She nodded.

"I can be a cop in New York."

"No. I'm not going to let you do that," she said, jumping to a sitting position. "This." She pointed back and forth between the two of them. "It's a trip down memory lane. It's a way for us to heal old wounds. It's not a path to a future together. Maybe if we'd been in touch this past year. Or maybe if we hadn't been so toxic when we broke up. But you and me, we're over."

"Are we?"

"Yes," she said softly. "And if you didn't think so before, you will after I tell you this."

"I'm listening," he said.

"I had a miscarriage a couple of weeks after I left last year."

"You had a what?" He swallowed his breath. "You were pregnant? With my baby?"

"Our baby, but yes." She held up her hand. "I didn't know until about a week after I landed in San Francisco, and I lost the baby about two and a half weeks after that."

His heart hammered in his chest. "Fuck, Callie. And if you hadn't miscarried? Would you have told me?"

"Of course I would have, but that doesn't change the facts. We're not meant to be together."

"That's bullshit." He shouldn't use sex to prove a point, but it was all that he had right now. He tilted her chin with his thumb and index finger. "I'm sorry about the baby. I really am. I wish I could have been there for you." Her lips parted, and her pupils widened. "But if our story ended, then why are we here in this bed about to make love?" He didn't give her a chance to respond. His mouth took hers in a hot, hard kiss that had only one intention and that was to devour.

He pressed his body against hers, letting her know exactly the power she held over him and what little control he had when it came to being in her presence. Of course, if she pushed him away, he'd leave the bed like the gentleman that he was, but by the way her tongue commanded his and the way her fingers dug into his ass cheeks, he suspected she wanted it as much as he did.

"Jag," she managed between raspy breaths.

"What, babe?"

"I'm a selfish woman."

"Why do you say that?" He slipped his hand under her shirt, removing the cotton fabric. He inhaled sharply, staring at her perfect small round breasts with tightly puckered pink nipples. Her chest rose up and down, presenting them to him.

"Because I'll gladly have sex with you for my own personal gratification, even though I don't want to hurt you."

He kissed the underswell of her breast. "What makes you think I'm worried about that? I'm a big boy, and you've made it clear that you think we're over."

She cupped his face. "Jag. We are. This is just sex. I'm sorry. If you can't... oh, my God." She arched her back while he slipped his finger inside her, curling gently, stroking tenderly. "That's not fair."

He chuckled. "First. When you and I are together, it can never be described as just sex. Second. Never be sorry about us. And finally, I want you to know that I will always respect your wishes, just as I did when you left the last time. You asked me not to chase after you. So I didn't. If, when you leave again, and you tell me this is over, I'll respect that."

She blinked a few times, licking her lips. "I… can't… respond," she said with a gasp. "When you're doing that."

"Do you want me to stop?"

"Hell no," she said, grabbing his forearm and encouraging him to dive deeper, harder, and faster.

He smiled as he leaned in and sucked her nipple into his mouth. She'd always been a wildcat, and their sex life had never been boring. Even what some might consider mundane lovemaking could only be described as passionate and desperate. She made him want to please her first, and if he never climaxed, it wouldn't matter.

Her desire was all that he cared about.

And his was all she ever focused on.

It was a sexual pairing made in what could only be described as a devilish heaven.

With sensitive hands, he removed her thong as well as his sweatpants and underwear. He made sure to take his time kissing every inch of her glorious body. He wanted to feel all her muscles twitch and shake under his touch. Perspiration dotted their skin like precious beads.

The light of the moon danced across the night sky, casting a glow over Puget Sound.

He kissed his way down her taut stomach, enjoying every soft curve and sweet moan. She tasted like warm honey. Her slender fingers threaded through his hair, guiding him to where she needed it most. It was easy to get lost in her pleasure, and there wasn't any other place he'd rather be.

She was home.

She lifted her hips. "Oh, Jag," she whispered.

Wanting to feel her climax tighten around him, he eased himself into her, kissing her tenderly.

She accepted his weight as if they were one person. Their bodies moved together in perfect harmony. Their soft moans filled the room, adding to the music.

They were made for each other, and he would

spend the next few days showing her just how much they should be together.

"I love you," he whispered in her ear while her body convulsed and shivered. He soaked up her orgasm before releasing his own.

"Jag," she said. "It's not that I don't. It's just that saying it will only make leaving harder."

He squeezed his eyes tight. "I know, babe. It's okay." He kissed her temple. Letting her go again was going to kill him.

10

The acid in Jag's stomach churned. He couldn't even take a sip of his coffee; his belly was so sour. He made the turn down Park Avenue, and as much as he wanted to deny reality, he knew deep down the Trinket Killer had returned.

He pulled into the brand-new glamping site and parked behind Jenna's patrol car. Also at the crime scene was Hanson Paget, one of his other officers.

Jag put the Jeep in park and surveyed the area. There were six glamping tents with one game tent, a tiki bar, firepit, and an outdoor kitchen. Hanson stood by the kitchen area with a group of people while Jenna made her way from one of the tents toward Jag. He sucked in a deep breath and stepped from his SUV.

"Hey, Chief," Jenna said. "Sorry to have woken you up."

He took a quick glance at his Apple Watch. Callie would be up soon, and she wasn't going to be happy he left without waking her.

Especially when she reads the note.

"It had to be done," he said. "So, what do we have?"

"White female. Approximately twenty-five to thirty years of age. Long blond hair. Tall. Slender. And she had one of those raven things you showed me in her left hand."

He rubbed his temple. "Left hand? Not right?"

"Yup," Jenna said. "And it was the rose gold raven trinket."

"The dolphins had been gold at first, then silver. All in their right hand. The other girls had been mood rings on their left ring finger."

"What are you babbling about?" Jenna asked.

"Cases that might be connected."

"Okay. I get the connection with the dolphins. That would be the Trinket Killer. But what about mood rings?"

"I'll send you the files, but we found a case that

we thought was closed, but maybe it was the early work of the Trinket Killer, who might be a woman."

"That's an interesting twist," Jenna said. "I'd like to see what made you draw that conclusion."

"Since the fucking asshole decided to drop a body on our doorstep, I'll make sure you get everything," he said. "I want you taking lead anyway."

"The mainland's going to do that, and you know it. I've already called CSI and the medical examiner. They are in the front of the ferry line right now," Jenna said. "Oh, and before I forget, Albert's on his way."

Jag headed toward the tent where the body was found. "Why? This didn't happen in the city of Seattle."

"Nope. But since we're probably going to make the connection to the Trinket Killer, he wants to be involved."

"Why him?" Not that he minded working with Albert. If anything, he'd prefer him. He just wanted to know why and how it happened so quickly.

"Don't get mad, Chief, but I called him directly first. I thought you'd want to get ahead of this just in case we really are dealing with that bastard again." Jenna stopped at the base of the tent platform and looped her fingers in her uniform belt.

"That was smart. Thanks. Now tell me everything I need to know." He sucked in a deep breath and tentatively ducked under the crime scene tape. The body lay on her back with her head tilted to the side. Her long hair haphazardly covered her face. Her left arm stretched out to the side, and her right one was draped over her stomach. She wore a pair of jeans, cowboy boots, and a thick white sweater now stained with blood from where she'd been stabbed.

Everything about the scene was identical to ten of the other Trinket Killer's victims.

The ten that he's decided the killer didn't care as much about because the kills weren't as violent nor did the killer take the extra steps of cleaning up and presenting the body.

Nope. All he—she did was make sure the trinket was placed in the hand.

"Our victim, Barbara Quinn, checked in at around six in the evening. Her girlfriend was supposed to meet her here around nine, but she never showed."

"Where is the girlfriend now?"

"We don't know," Jenna said. "We believe her

name is Holly Whalen and that our victim just met her a couple of weeks ago."

"Was she already on the island?"

"According to the owners of the glamping site, when Barbara checked in, she said her new girlfriend was coming from the mainland. Hanson is still interviewing everyone. Barbara was quite friendly and spent some time at the tiki bar with a bottle of wine. One of the guests said she was pretty tipsy when she went to bed at midnight."

Jag arched a brow. "And what did she have to say about her new girlfriend and her ETA? The ferry only runs until one in the morning."

"Same guest said Holly finally texted back stating something came up and she'd call in the morning."

"Ouch," Jag said as he knelt by the body, snapping on a pair of gloves. He took a pen and lifted up a thick clump of hair. "The victim has bruises and a cut on her cheek. Looks like maybe a scratch from a fingernail."

"That's what I was thinking. There are some on her wrist as well," Jenna said.

"If she fought back, how the hell did no one hear?" he mumbled.

"The couple in the tent next door heard something. They don't know what woke them up. They said they heard a thud, like something falling."

"Or a body hitting the ground."

"Yeah. But, Chief, I don't think she was killed here."

"Why do you say that?"

"They heard that at about two and went back to sleep. The husband then heard a rustling noise and the sound of a zipper. He said he saw a shadow race out of the tent. A few minutes later he heard the sound of an engine down the road. He decided to check things out, and he found Barbara on the floor. That was at four twelve."

"So, you think the killer came into the tent, they left, fought, and then the killer murdered our victim somewhere else and dragged the body back here."

"I do. Look at the back of the tent," Jenna said.

Jag lifted his gaze. The flaps were pulled down, and the screen wasn't zipped all the way up.

"It's freezing at night out here. You don't leave those suckers down and turn the space heaters too low. You won't stay warm. I know this from experience. My husband and I stay here every time he's back from a deployment. I was too lazy one night after using the outhouse, and my husband cussed me out something good when I made him get his sorry naked ass out of bed to both zip it up and turn the heaters on full blast."

Jag chuckled. Knowing her husband, he could only imagine what came out of that sailor's mouth. Of course, Jenna gave as good as she got. "Any blood?"

"There is some on the floor and on the bed," Jenna said. "But if you look under her body, there is very little. Another reason why I don't think she was killed here."

"She could have gotten up to use the bathroom and was taken out there," Jag said. "It didn't have to originate here, and I don't see signs of a struggle inside the tent."

"Good point."

Jag turned his attention to the left hand and the trinket.

A raven.

Rose gold.

Placed in the palm.

"Oh fuck," he mumbled.

"What is it?" Jenna asked, standing behind him.

"It's a mood ring on her left finger."

Jag took a step back while the medical examiner zipped up the body bag and placed it on the gurney. He followed Albert out of the tent and toward the kitchen area.

Jenna and Hanson had finished up with the rest of the guests, taking their information, and were currently helping to escort them off the property. The glamping site would be shut down for at least the next couple of days.

"Let's take a walk around the grounds again," Albert said, slipping off his gloves and tossing them in the trash. "Thank you for letting me help."

Jag laughed. "I had a choice?"

"Not really," Albert said. "But you do realize that's the first time the Trinket Killer has left the city of Seattle."

"That we know of," Jag added. "But that brings up something I was thinking about this morning."

"Don't hurt yourself with all that brain power."

Jag stepped behind one of the tents and onto a trail that looped around the property and through a couple of hiking trails. "I had originally thought that when we released Adam it gave our killer permission to finish her cycle."

"You're really sold the killer is a woman?"

"I am," Jag said. "I really believe she would

have killed Stephanie anyway. There was no pause when we caught Adam, and I think we should take a look at his murder a little more closely. The Trinket Killer could have murdered him for a plethora of different reasons."

"I've already pulled the case."

"Thanks." Jag walked slowly down the path, scanning a few feet left and right, looking for clues of any kind. "So, I was thinking that if victims with the mood rings is the Trinket Killer, she didn't stop when we caught the janitor. But since he wasn't released, and the world thought he'd done it, she might have switched up her game."

"That's a solid reason for a serial killer to change their MO."

"Which means, we're looking for three dead young women with blond hair, killed sometime between the last Mood Ring murder and the first dolphin one."

"Have you noticed the victims haven't aged that much over the course of fifteen years when all this started?" Albert asked.

"I have. The Mood Ring victims were all younger than twenty. The dolphin victims were under the age of twenty-five, except Stephanie. She was just a year older."

"But you know what's weird?" Albert asked.

"What?"

"Normally, when we see this, we think our unsub is killing the same person over and over. But this feels like there is a shift with each trinket or color."

"I have to agree with you," Jag said. "And the change of right or left hand. And I believe even more now that Renee and Stephanie knew their killer." Jag paused just as they came to the clearing on the other side of the property. He turned and faced his longtime friend. "I want to pull Callie into the conversation."

"You're joking, right?" Albert asked as he folded his arms across his chest. "She's writing a fucking tell-all book."

"Not even close. And let me tell you, I've read what she's written so far, and some of my conclusions that we've just discussed have come from her research. She's smart, and she'd be a huge asset. Besides, she's not working for the station anymore. As a civilian, she can do things we can't."

Albert wiggled his index finger in his ear. "I'm going to pretend you didn't just say that because I'd hate to see you get fired."

Jag tried not to laugh because it wasn't funny.

Ajax and Albert had gone out on a limb for Jag more than once.

And they'd do it again, as would Jag.

"I would like to keep this as quiet as possible," Albert said. "We don't need the press bringing up the Trinket Killer."

"That I'm on board with, but how are we going to do that when the Feds have been called in?"

"The agent in charge is going to be very low-key and stay in the background, but we absolutely don't want the public to think the Trinket Killer is back," Albert said. "How do you feel about taking a calculated risk?"

"I've been doing that my entire career. Why would I stop now?"

"Good." Albert slapped him on the shoulder. "I'm sure the press will be out here eventually. Mind telling them we've got a person of interest that we're talking to?"

"Do we?" Jag arched a brow. It wouldn't be the first time something like this happened. "Because if we're going to play the I'm just the local small-town cop, and you're the big badass city slicker, and you're going to go do shit behind my—"

"Relax, Jag. I know how personal this is for you, and I wouldn't dream of doing that to you." Albert glanced in the direction where Jenna and Hanson stood. "We have a series of dating murders, and our killer only communicates with us when we get something wrong. We're so close to catching him, and if I link this to him, he might contact me. In the meantime, that gets people like Bailey off your back while you dig to your heart's content and hopefully turn over something that will finally, after fucking years, give us a goddamned answer on this one."

"Do what you need to."

"All right. I've got to get back to the mainland. I'll be in touch."

Jag stood at the edge of the woods with his hands on his hips and stared at the fog slinking through the air, hiding the morning sun, leaving a misty dew on the grass.

Now all he had to do was tell Callie he would investigate with her.

11

Callie sat behind Jag's desk in his home office and flipped through the Mood Ring victim files for the eighth time. In all the time she'd been dating Jag, and they pretended to investigate together, they had always kept each other at a safe distance.

He actually had to because of his job.

Her job required her to do whatever it took to get the story, including beg, borrow, steal, or lie.

And she did.

Which is what, in part, destroyed their relationship.

Something she had to come to terms with. Of course, he did his share of sabotaging their future, but right now, he was taking measures to rebuild.

While she was still backpedaling.

"You look like your mind is turning something over," Jag said.

"No. That's my stomach telling me to vomit." She swallowed the tiny bit of bile that kept bubbling up her throat. "If your theory is correct, then the first kill is always violent. The one yesterday at the glamping site while horrific, wasn't that brutal."

"I know. I thought about that too." Jag sat in a leather chair across the room with his feet up on a footstool while he tossed a tiny football up in the air. He used to do that when he'd been deep in thought, working a case that was making him lose sleep.

And last night, if he'd gotten more than three hours, it would have been a miracle.

A tap at the door startled her and she jumped, knocking over one of the files.

Ziggy opened the door and set a tray of food on the table by the door. "I'm heading back to Seattle. I'll see you two later."

"Thanks, sis," Jag said as he blew her a kiss. "Say hello to Mom and Dad. Tell them I'll call them later."

"Please tell me you're going to come tonight," Ziggy said.

"I don't know." Jag continued to toss the football. "I'm a little swamped right now."

"You're off duty, technically until tomorrow morning at eight," Ziggy said.

"I'm never off duty as chief," Jag said. "And I just don't know that I'm in a family dinner kind of mood. Besides, I don't want to leave—"

"She's still considered family." She pointed at Callie. "So bring her."

"Oh, no." Callie lifted one of the home-baked cookies off the tray and took a bite. It was still warm. Best damn cookies she'd ever had. "Last time I saw your dad, he gave me the famous Bowie look of disappointment. It still haunts me."

Ziggy clutched her chest. "If you don't come, he might hunt you down just to give you the look, which you really haven't seen yet. That was just his sad, please don't go look."

"He saves that for Darcie," Jag said. "Did I tell you she's living on a sailboat now?"

"That I didn't know," Callie said. "But it doesn't surprise me. Darcie has always had a love for the sea. I'm actually shocked she's not living the Yachtie lifestyle."

"She's close." Ziggy laughed. "So, I'll tell Mom

and Dad you'll both be there for dinner." With that, Ziggy closed the door.

"You should go have dinner with your family," Callie said.

"If I go, you're coming with me."

She rolled her eyes. "Why? Other than Ziggy, they all hate me for the way I left."

He shook his head. "They resent me for not chasing after you."

She stared at him for a long moment, holding his intense gaze. She'd dated him for months before he told his family. For the most part, they'd all been accepting of her and willing to keep their relationship quiet. Once he caught the Trinket Killer, then they'd be able to slowly let the world know about their love.

"If I go without you, they will think I'm being a dick as usual."

"God forbid anyone think badly of you," she said, trying to lighten the mood, though it was impossible while staring at a bunch of cold cases.

"I really only worry about what you think of me, but please, I want you to come, and I'm sure my family does too."

"I'll think about it. Now can we get back to this?"

"Absolutely," he said, settling back down in the chair with his football, a couple of cookies, and a mug of coffee.

Callie reopened the file and started reading again, comparing the first Mood Ring crime scene to Renee's. "On the surface, it's hard to make the mood killer and Renee's killer the same."

"Why?"

"The weapon, for one."

"The first kill might have been the trigger for everything else," Jag said. "Whatever happened between our killer and the victim caused the unsub to snap. She kills and goes right into perfecting the kill the way she wished she'd done it the first time. And look at the pattern of how the victim was beaten." Jag jumped to his feet and shuffled through a few of the papers before shoving some images in front of her face.

She inhaled sharply, trying not to hurl. She'd seen dead bodies before. She'd examined crime scene evidence. This was nothing new.

But it all took on new meaning now that the Trinket Killer had returned.

"There's a distinct pattern in the stab wounds with Renee and Stephanie. They are similar with the bludgeon marks on vic number one with the mood rings. And come on, body presentation is all the same."

"And different from all the other victims," Callie said, holding up her hand, knowing he was going to go down a road they'd traveled way too many times, and it was starting to make her head hurt. "Thing is the killer had to know all her victims."

"Why do you say that?" Jag flattened his hands on the desk and leaned over.

Methodically, she laid out all the victims, except for the ones that had been brutal. "Each one was murdered while waiting to meet someone." She tapped victim number four. "According to the bartender who had last seen her, she was waiting for a friend who didn't show up." Callie lifted the picture of victim number seven. "According to eyewitnesses, she was waiting at a coffee shop for a friend. No one knows who that friend was. I bet if we go through all of these, we will find every single woman was waiting on a friend who happened to be a female that was new to their lives."

"Just like Stephanie had a new girlfriend whom we hadn't met yet." Jag let out a long breath. "But that sort of blows my theory because I thought the violence had to do with caring about the victim. I mean, I was thinking that if Renee had cheated a second time, her lover might be a jealous bitch or something. And since then has been killing women who are like Renee, and we both know how excited Stephanie was over this new woman."

"She was very excited," Callie said. "But the night she was murdered, she was desperate to talk to me. To us. And that's always struck me as odd."

"Why?"

"Because it wasn't just me she wanted to see. But she specifically said she needed to speak with you. She said I had to bring you."

"Yeah. I remember the voicemail. But I'm not sure I'm following your train of thought here."

"Stephanie was on her way to see us. She wasn't going to meet 'a friend.'"

"That then blows the theory we've been forming."

She shook her head. "I believe our theory is still correct. The violence is out of anger. Our killer is mad as hell at the people they love the most. She kills them brutally. Beating them or stabbing them. Or both. Then they take the time to clean the body. Brush their hair, fix their makeup. Hell, even in Renee's case, the killer tried to do something with the poor woman's face."

"Renee was found at her favorite beach."

"My sister at her favorite park."

"All right, so that gives us some questions to ask."

"Some are already answered." She pushed a piece of paper at him. "One of the victims' siblings stated they found it strange that their sister was found by the community pool because she couldn't swim but always wanted to learn."

"Interesting."

"I think the killer had to have at least known each woman for a minimum of a week before killing them. In some cases longer, especially the ones who were bi or gay."

"Are you now thinking these are sexually motivated?" Jag asked.

"I don't know. I think so, but maybe not in the way we think since she's killing straight women as well."

"They could have turned her down," Jag said. "But that probably would have made her angry, increasing the violence."

"There is one other thing that really jumped at me today, looking through all this stuff."

"What's that?"

"Armstrong."

"What about her?"

"She looks an awful lot like the victims." Callie shuffled through the papers and found the pictures of Leslie Armstrong taken over her years of service.

"What are you talking about? She was a brunette, and she was well into her fifties if not sixty when she killed herself."

"She was fifty-eight," Callie said. "And when she was in her thirties, she was a blonde." Callie flashed the image in front of Jag. "She changed her hair color, it seems, about five years before the start of the Trinket Killer."

"Jesus. She looks exactly like our... Fuck, she looks like you."

"Similar features, yes. And she tampered with evidence on an investigation where women who looked like her were being murdered. What do you make of that?" she asked.

He leaned over and planted a wet kiss on her lips. "You're a fucking genius."

"All I did was raise more questions than answers." She slumped in the chair, exhausted.

"You made connections and gave us lots of rocks to look under. I'm going to go call Albert. Why don't you go jump in the shower? I want to be on the five o'clock ferry to my folks."

She dropped her head to the desk with a thud.

"I'm only going because... because..." Why the hell was she going?

"Because you love me," he said.

She waved her hand in defeat. "Whatever you say." It was the truth, but again, the words would not be allowed to flow between her lips.

That would make it too real, and she'd never leave.

She had to leave.

Too many bad things happened in Seattle.

Jag hopped up on the kitchen counter and took a long swig of his beer. "How long are you here for?"

"Just a few days," his brother Troy said. Troy was a fighter pilot for the Navy, currently stationed at Pearl Harbor. "I'm sorry I didn't call. I wasn't sure I'd even be able to get here."

"Mom and Dad were sure shocked to see you," Jag said. "You need a place to crash?"

"Nah. I'll stay with the folks. Besides, Ziggy says you and Callie are all cozy again."

Jag tipped back his head, taking another sip of his beverage.

"You're not denying it."

Jag chuckled. "Cozy might be one way to describe it, but she plans on leaving as soon as she's done with her book."

"If that's the case, why the fuck are you letting her stay with you, much less share your bed?"

"It's complicated," Jag admitted.

"One of the many reasons why this sailor is never going to fall in love." Troy pulled open the fridge and pulled out a plate of leftovers. He was the third kid in the family, about two years younger than Ziggy. When Jag had been a senior in high school, Troy had been a freshman, and it had been frustrating as hell to have his baby brother make the varsity football team.

And then be a starter.

But they'd gone to states that year and won, and honestly, they couldn't have done it without the dynamic duo of Jag in the quarterback position and Troy as the main receiver.

Jag shouldn't feel so proud that his high school couldn't make it to states again for many years, but he did, just a little.

"Love isn't such a bad thing," Jag said.

"I'm sure it's not. I just don't have time for it, or all the bullshit that comes with it, especially in my career." He waved a chicken wing in the air. "Do you remember my buddy Alister?"

"You were his best man a couple of years ago."

"Yup. And he's getting divorced. Fucking sucks. Bitch wife of his cheated. I never liked her." Troy tore off a big chunk of chicken between his teeth. "But Callie, she's something special. I have to admit when I heard she was back, it made me smile, but not if she's going to break your heart again, especially over a tell-all book that makes you look incompetent."

"She didn't break it. I did," Jag corrected his little brother. "And for the record, I've read the draft. It actually puts me in a pretty good light, considering how I did fuck up the investigation."

Troy jumped up on the counter and shoved the plate of food between them. When they'd been growing up, they spent a lot of time in this kitchen, sitting on this very counter in the middle of the night, discussing anything and everything. They both cried over girls and fought over football. Despite the four-year age difference, Troy had always been one of his best friends, even if they acted like they hated each other half the time.

"No matter what anyone said about her when she first left, you always defended her," Troy said.

"She was in pain when she left. Other than me, her sister was all she had, and she had to blame someone. I made it real easy for her since I blamed myself." Jag tossed a chicken bone on the plate. "After she flipped out at the crime scene, I had to take her home. She cried in my arms for hours. We talked the next morning, and when I left, I said something so stupid that I knew right then I'd lost her."

"What did you say?"

"I think my exact words were something like, *'Stop playing Nancy Drew. You're not helping the situation. If anything, you're getting in my way.'*"

"Fuck, dude. You might as well have dumped her."

"I know," he said, rubbing his throbbing temples. "I've never told anyone, but the department shrink agreed. If Mom knew she'd—"

"Have your damn head?" his mother's voice rang out behind him.

He jumped right off the counter.

"You too, Troy. Off. Now." His mother poked Troy in the back with her long manicured fingernail. Henrietta Bowie was one tough cookie, and she didn't take shit from anyone, especially her kids. She ran a tight ship and demanded respect.

"Yes, ma'am," Troy said.

"Sorry, Mom." Jag wiped his fingers on a paper towel.

"For what? Putting your tushy on my counter or being a dickhead when it comes to the best thing that has ever happened to you?"

"Both," he admitted.

"Good." His mother patted his cheek with her palm. "Now tell me, what are you doing to get her back? Because if she walks out of our lives again, this mama bear isn't going to be so happy. And no one likes it when I'm miserable."

"I'm working on it," Jag said. "I hope the rest of this family isn't scaring her off. You all are part of the reason we kept our relationship a secret in the first place."

His mother laughed. "That's bullshit, and you know it."

"I'm with Mom on this one," Troy said, still waving around a chicken wing. The man never stopped eating. "It started off as a booty call."

"Troy Markus Bowie. Don't you dare refer to that amazing young woman as a booty call."

"But that's what she started out as." Troy tossed his hands to the sides.

"I'd prefer to think of it as Jag being her whatever call."

Jag laughed. "She did call me the first few times."

His mother smacked the back side of his head. Didn't stop him from laughing. While his parents raised him to be respectful, their family, when alone, had no filter.

And Mom was the worst.

"Let's forget the past," his mother said. "And tell me what your plan is."

"Oh, Mom. I can't tell you that," Jag said with a wicked grin.

His mother narrowed her eyes. "I already know she's sleeping in your bed, so that's a start, but satisfying a woman in the sack isn't going to keep her forever. That's just the icing on the cake."

Troy snagged another beer. "That's my cue to leave."

"Mine too," Jag said.

"You're not going anywhere." His mom gave him a good shove in the back. "Take a seat at the table." She poured herself a glass of white wine and handed him another beer.

"Mom. I love you. But I'm a grown-ass man. I don't need help with my love life."

"Do you really want to reconcile?" She reached across the table and took him by the hand. "And I mean a long-term reconciliation as in give her the ring back?"

He glanced over his shoulder. "She doesn't know I found it, so please don't say anything."

"I won't. Now answer my question."

"You're worse than me in an interrogation room."

His mother smiled like she'd just won the lottery.

He let out a long breath. "Yes. I want her back in a forever way."

"Have you told her how you feel?"

"She knows I still love her, and yes, she still loves me." He held up his hand when his mother started to smile. "But she doesn't think we have a chance in hell and plans on leaving in a couple of weeks."

"I see. So what are you doing, besides assuming sex solves everything?"

"I'm listening to her, something I didn't do last year when it came to her instincts about certain things."

His mother nodded. "The murder out on the island today. Why is she looking into…" His mom's words trailed off as her eyes went wide.

"You don't believe that the Trinket Killer is back, do you?"

"I can't talk about that with you."

"That's cop speak for yes."

"It's not a yes." He lowered his gaze. "But it's not a no either."

"Understood," his mother said. "But that scares me, especially with her being back. Stephanie, outside of you, was her entire world."

"I know. And I let them both down." Thick emotion clung to his throat, making it difficult to swallow. "I'm doing everything I can think of to make it up to her and show her that I've changed. That I'm not the same arrogant asshole that belittled her theories and lied to her."

"Now, you I know I love that girl. And I want the two of you to work this out. But has she changed?"

He nodded. "But she's jaded, and she's built a wall around her so high that it's going to take some doing on my part to knock it down, and the clock is ticking."

"You said she's staying until she finishes the book. But if this thing you can't talk about is connected, won't that change the time she will need to complete the project?"

"It might. But that could also cause a new rift. Right now, I'm giving her full disclosure, which could get me fired. The thing is, I'm not doing it to get her back. I'm doing it because she's smarter than me, and she's onto something, and I need her help."

"So tell her that."

"I plan on it, but the timing has to be just right." He lifted his mom's hand and kissed the back of it. "I'm not going to let her go this time without a fight."

12

Callie took off her computer glasses and set them aside. She lifted her laptop off her legs and put it on the coffee table. Her gaze shifted between city hall and Puget Sound. The edge of the sun kissed the mountains, and the sky exploded into a swarm of purples, oranges, pinks, and reds dancing over the ripples of the water.

"What a view," she whispered. She could get used to island life, especially in this little gem of a house with a master suite that had the best little porch ever. There were no homes behind Jag's, so he didn't block anyone else's view of the sound.

She picked up her cell. It was close to four in the afternoon. Jag had left for the office at six. He'd texted her a few times and told her he'd probably make it back by five or five thirty. Not that she was a needy woman and made any kind of demands on any man she'd ever dated.

But she was going stir-crazy and cross-eyed between writing and research.

Callie: *How's work?*

Instead of staring at the phone waiting for the bubbles to pop up, she dropped her head back and sucked in a deep breath. For some reason, the air on the islands in Puget Sound had a denseness to it. It wasn't harsh, like trying to take a deep breath near a smoke-filled city. It was more like the salt and fog clashing together making a thicker, fresher air that expanded her lungs in a way that no other place could.

Ding.

She smiled, lifting her cell.

Jag: *Unusually busy today. Lost dog. Bicycling accident. House fire. And a lego stuck in a teenager's nose. Don't ask.*

She laughed.

Callie: *Where are you?*

Jag: *Headed up to Beverly Beach.*

Callie: *Why?*

Jag: *About to get in patrol car. Got to go. I'll text when I'm on my way home.*

Fucker. He used to love doing that to her,

knowing she'd never keep texting once she knew he was in a moving vehicle. Usually, whatever call he was heading out on wasn't anything for her to worry about, so she set her phone down. Her computer screen daunted her. She'd written five thousand words, which was close to half the chapter dedicated to Jag. It was easier to write than she thought in the sense that so much of the anger she'd been hanging on to for the last year had evaporated, unlike the constant fog that Seattle lived under. That allowed her to look at Jag a little more objectively.

But it was also harder because a different set of raw emotions bubbled to the surface. Deep down, she'd always known she still had feelings for Jag, but she'd buried them in a dark corner of her mind, never allowing her heart to acknowledge her one true love.

Jag.

She reached out and lifted her computer, clicking on a folder labeled: *Stephanie*. Tears burned the corners of Callie's eyes.

Her childhood had been picture-perfect. She and Stephanie grew up in the suburbs of Seattle with loving parents. Her father was a heart surgeon, and her mother was a nurse in the emergency room. They were the perfect power couple, and when Stephanie, at a very young age, started transitioning, her folks were right there with her every step of the way. They never judged, even though it was obvious they struggled at first.

They had to grieve the loss of their son, in a way, but always knew they loved their child, no matter if she called herself Steven or Stephanie.

She clicked on the last family portrait that had been taken just three weeks before her parents were killed in a helicopter crash while transporting a high-risk, high-profile heart patient.

Everyone on board died.

Callie reached out and touched her father's face. And then her mother's. Tears now scorched her cheeks. They had died two years before Stephanie was murdered. "I miss you all," Callie whispered.

While Jag didn't fill a void in her heart, he certainly helped her out of a dark place after she'd lost her parents.

Her phone rang.

FaceTime from Kara.

She smiled and clicked the accept tab on her computer, setting it up on the table as she slouched in the chair. "Hey, Kara. How are you?"

"I'm doing good. How's my Callie girl?"

Callie wondered if Kara heard about the murder on the island. It hadn't made national news, because the cops had successfully suppressed any potential connection it might have to the Trinket Killer. Hell, it barely made the local news, except for Bailey, who enjoyed reporting that it was unsolved and that Jag was the chief of police, as if it was expected he would solve the murder within minutes of it happening.

"I'm hanging tough." Callie tucked a stray strand of hair behind her ear as she pulled her fleece tighter around her chest. "Where are you?"

"We're still in Oregon. It's beautiful here."

"I bet. Are you in a hotel?" Callie leaned forward, trying to get a better look, but it was hard to make out the details on the tiny screen.

"We're staying in an Airbnb."

"Where's Ivy?"

"She's in the shower. We went for a fifteen-mile walk today. I'm so sore." Kara lay on a bed on her stomach with her face propped up by her hand. She was a good ten years older than Callie and often acted slightly maternal, and that tended to annoy Callie, but it was nice to have someone care that much.

"I'm going to end up finishing the book early," Callie said. "Jag's been great."

"I have to admit I'm shocked by that," Kara said. "I know he's not a bad man, nor is he a bad cop. It's just that he said some things to you that you just can't take back."

"I said some things too," Callie said. "But at the end of the day, I still love him."

"But is he good for you?" Kara moved to a sitting position, leaning against a headboard. "And is Seattle good for you?"

"Seattle, not so much. But I like island life."

Kara laughed. "You're sleeping with him, aren't you?"

"That's none of your business."

"Oh, Callie girl." Kara shook her head. "I was worried that would happen if you stayed out on that island. I'm concerned about you."

"I know and I'm fine. Really. I am. Things are good. I've made it clear that I'm leaving in a couple of weeks. He understands that. This is just a nice way for us to get the closure we never had before."

"What does he say?"

It was rare that Callie lied to Kara, and she was going to do it twice in one phone call. Once by omission, since she wasn't going to tell her anything about the murder.

And once right now.

"He agrees with me."

Kara cocked her head, and her lips parted. "Are you serious?"

Callie nodded, making sure she kept her smile steady and her gaze locked on the screen. "Being in close quarters, sleeping together was inevitable. I mean, the sex was always fucking mind-blowing, and it's been a long time since I've been with a man."

"Maybe you should try a woman," Kara said with a tongue-in-cheek tone.

"Now you sound like my sister."

A sobering silence settled between them. They stared at each other for a few moments. Kara hadn't known her sister that well, but she'd been Callie's rock.

"Oh, before I forget," Kara said. "Ivy thought of something when it comes to the ravens."

"Yeah. What's that?"

"A spirit animal. Interestingly enough, when I gave her some information about you, she thought the raven was your spirit animal."

"That's weird."

"That's what I thought, but she's putting together an entire thing on it. When she's done, I'll send it to you."

"Thanks. I appreciate it." Callie's pulse kicked up. Perhaps the killer thought the dolphin and now the raven was her spirit animal. Or represented whoever the killer was murdering over and over again, if that was indeed the motive. She quickly opened her research folder and made a note to research that concept more thoroughly.

A Langley police car turned the bend in front of Jag's house.

"Kara. I've got to go. Say hello to Ivy for me."

"Will do. Love you, Callie girl." Kara blew a kiss before the screen turned dark.

Callie set the computer to the side and stood, watching Jenna step from the driver's seat.

"Hi, Callie, how are you?"

"I'm okay," she called from the second-story deck. "Did Jag send you to check on me?"

Jenna shook her head. "He sent me to tell you he's going to be late."

"Why?"

"A body was found over at Beverly Beach. It was brutal. The sheriff's office was the first on the scene.

When they called Jag for help, they didn't give him all the details."

Callie clutched her chest. It hurt to breathe. "What did Jag find when he got there?"

"He thinks it's the first kill for this cycle," Jenna said.

The city of Langley was more like a small town. It didn't cover a lot of space on Whidbey Island, and his jurisdiction was generally limited, but the sheriff's office often relied on Jag's support.

And he never said no.

But a second dead body on the island within a couple of days of each other?

That never happened.

"What exactly did DeSantis say?" Jag rested his elbow on the open window. The chilly spring air filled the patrol car, cooling his nerves.

Jenna punched the gas, turning down Beach Drive. "A body was found in an Airbnb this afternoon after a neighbor complained about the smell. The rental had been secured for the entire month, so no one was checking on it."

"Who actually found the body?" Jag asked.

"The landlord used his key when no one came to the door. The body was presented on the bed."

"I don't like how you used that word."

Jenna adjusted her shades, which was funny because the sun wasn't very strong this afternoon. "I'm only repeating what DeSantis said."

"What do you think?"

Jenna glanced in his direction. "That your girlfriend stirred up some shit, and the killer isn't happy she's back."

"This isn't her fault," Jag said with a tight jaw.

"No shit, Chief," Jenna said. "I was saying that maybe she's a trigger for a killer that she spent the majority of her career covering, but mostly I wanted to hear you admit she's your girlfriend."

"Five years, to be exact." He chose to ignore the girlfriend comment. He could only hope that were the case. "But we also have to consider that it's more likely we have a copycat."

"Agreed," Jenna said as she parked the police vehicle behind the sheriff's car.

Jag stretched before he made his way up the walkway toward where DeSantis and two other uniformed officers stood.

"Jesus," Jenna muttered, covering her mouth and nose.

Jag did the same.

"Thanks for coming," Officer Carlos DeSantis said with an outstretched hand.

"Happy to help," Jag said. "How long do we think the body has been in there?"

"It was rented on the eighth of the month," DeSantis said.

"That was the day before Ajax's going away party," Jag said.

"What does that have to do with anything?" Jenna asked.

"Probably nothing." Jag planted his hands on his hips and scanned the immediate area, trying to get a feel for the neighborhood. Of course, he'd been in this general area many times. It was a quiet seaside town, just like every little place on Whidbey. "Just grounding myself." He turned his head and took a deep breath of fresh air. "All right. Let's get this over with."

"Follow me," DeSantis said. "I've called in the medical examiner and CSI. They are en route. I thought I'd wait to call Seattle PD until I talked to you since you were the lead on most of the Trinket Killer cases."

He'd come out to the island to get away from all the insanity that the Trinket Killer had brought to his life, and he'd thought he found a nice quiet little life for himself.

So much for carefully laid plans.

Of course, he thought he'd be married by now with maybe a baby on the way.

Wishful thinking.

He pulled his dark shirt up over his mouth. There were no words to describe a corpse. People tried, using words like rotten eggs. Or urine-soaked clothes left out in the sun for days.

The stench was ten times worse than both of those combined, and it filled your lungs, clinging to the sides, taking hours to expel.

Jenna held the department camera and snapped a few pictures as they made their way to the back bedroom.

"The body was laid out on the bed. Left arm stretched out and right arm resting over the midsection. Head is turned slightly to the left. The victim's long blond hair has been brushed and styled," DeSantis said.

Jag could have done without constant commentary. He stepped into the bedroom and did his best not to breathe. He stepped to the left side of the bed and leaned over.

Sure enough, there was a rose gold raven trinket

in the left hand, and the victim was wearing a mood ring.

And the victim's face was bashed in, so he couldn't even get an image to run through a recognition program.

All the other women had been twisted to their right, not left. Their bodies weren't shaped exactly the same way.

Except for Renee and Stephanie, who also had impeccable hair.

But the one thing he noticed about Stephanie's was that it wasn't a style she would normally wear. Kara had said Renee's hair was the way she wore it all the time.

He was going to have to compare hair styles of the living.

A memory tickled the back of his brain. He recalled Callie mentioning something about the hairstyles during one of their fights.

But did she mention it in the book?

Come to think of it, he didn't think she had.

Why not?

A wave of nausea gripped his gut. He turned and took long strides toward the front door, Jenna and DeSantis riding on his heels. A million things raced through his mind, but he couldn't make sense of them.

All he knew was that somehow the hair was connected, and it all led back to Renee somehow.

He glanced over his shoulder. Albert had rolled his vehicle to a stop in front of the house, just behind the CSI unit.

"Jenna, I need you to do me a favor."

"What's that, Chief?"

"Go to my place and tell Callie to pull up headshots of all our victims, even the ones from the Mood Ring cases. She'll know what those are. Have her compare hair styles both while alive and then the crime scenes." He scratched at the center of his chest.

"You don't believe that this is a copycat at all, do you?" Jenna asked.

"Nope," he admitted. "And I think you were dead on in the car on the way over here. Only, I don't think Callie was a trigger. I think our killer has been waiting patiently for her return."

"Do you think she's on his list to be murdered?"

He swallowed.

Hard.

If the theory he was forming in his brain was correct, Callie could easily be one of the victims just based on her looks, but something told him that she was more connected to these girls than even she knew.

Than even he suspected.

But what the fuck was the connection?

13

Callie hated taking over Jag's office, but she needed to compare her information with as much of the police files as he was willing to give her.

"I didn't want to be right about the hair," she mumbled as she pinned another image on the corkboard he'd bought her on the way home from the crime scene.

Jag leaned his ass against the desk, curling his fingers around the sides. "For the record, I believed you when you said it after Stephanie died, but you never let me tell you that."

"I thought the hair on the other women, while not styled, was manipulated a little to look a certain way." She joined him on the desk. "Did you have any luck finding cases like the Mood Ring ones?"

"Albert did." Jag held up his finger and twisted his body while he found his tablet on a desk filled with files. "He sent me nine possible. I ruled out all but two, with a third being iffy; however, feel free to take a look at all of them."

She glanced at him with an arched brow. "Are we questioning our instincts?"

"No. I've just learned not to question yours."

She bit back a smile as she scrolled through the information. Every murder that Albert had sent was a white female under the age of twenty-one who had been found in a park or campsite and had something in her left hand.

Two of them had what were known as mood stones. The rest were necklaces or pictures or other objects, except one.

She zoomed in on one image that had no trinket at the scene, but met every other criteria, as well as the girl having gone to the same college as the first three victims of the Mood Ring Killer, only the body had been found in her dorm, and it hadn't been staged.

Her face had also been beaten.

Callie flipped back to the other two cases.

Both girls attended the same college.

Jag glanced over her shoulder. "I was looking at the same three." He tapped at the screen. "This one. Victoria Patterson is the victim's name. I obviously haven't had time to read everything, but doesn't it feel like the killer was interrupted?"

"It does. And since the face was beaten, the hair should have been done, but it wasn't."

"And the evidence points to her being killed in the dorm. Other than your sister and Renee, the other victims were moved."

"Not the first Mood Ring Killer victim," Callie said. "Can you print those out so I can pin them?"

"Of course."

"Six is the sign of the devil." Callie handed him the tablet and stared at the wall of victims. "Ravens usually mean a bad omen or death. But I don't get dolphins or mood rings."

"Maybe we're attacking that from the wrong angle," he said.

"What do you mean?"

"I think we need to look to the victims for the meaning of the trinkets." He stepped closer to the corkboard. "Mood Ring victim number one was a lesbian. As was dolphin trinket with the gold and then with the silver."

"My sister was trans but identified as a lesbian," Callie said, rubbing her temples. "But then that should have reset the killer's cycle."

"Not necessarily. Not if the number six means something. And maybe the killer would have kept going." Jag found one of the raven trinkets on the desk. "Maybe she just would have gone to rose gold trinkets."

"Okay. But why smash in my sister's face when the Trinket Killer didn't do that to number six?"

"I'm going to go out on a limb here and suggest that the killer might have been intimate with those she became overly violent with."

"I could be on board with that. But why stop the killing for a year?" Callie was so tired of the same questions. No matter how much new information they uncovered, the same fundamental answers needed to solve this mystery were nowhere to be found.

"Well, let's look at the timeline. Renee was murdered, what, about six years ago?"

Callie nodded.

"The first Mood Ring Killer victim was murdered fourteen years ago. Neither Albert nor Marlo from the cold case division could find anything in Seattle or the surrounding areas that come close. I've called a buddy I know in the FBI, and he's going through their database. But we could be looking at a fourteen-year break."

Callie turned, pulling out the chair. She pushed through a bunch of the papers and files. She wasn't quite sure what she was looking for, but her brain told her she needed to find what pulled them all together, and she knew the connection was in this stack somewhere.

It had to be.

"Who found Patterson's body?" Callie asked.

"I didn't get that far. I think I might have been ten years old when those murders happened. I don't remember them at all."

"Why would you at that age?" Callie said. She found the file and scanned it. "It says her roommate found the body. The officer first on the scene reported that she entered the room, saw the body, and freaked out, running down the hall, screaming for someone to call 9-1-1."

"She didn't stay to see if her roommate was alive or to perform CPR?"

"Not according to the report," Callie said, holding up the case file she remembered reading, and a few things jumped out at her. "Another interesting thing is the victim didn't die until about an hour after she got to the hospital."

"So, it's possible that either the roommate did it or the roommate walked in and saw something."

"That's what I thought," Callie said. "The roommate said she didn't see anything but the body on the floor. She did say the door was locked and that was rare when they were in the room on a Wednesday afternoon. Also, the dorm room was on the first floor and the window was open, so the killer could have escaped that way when the roommate was trying to get in."

"Who was the roommate?" Jag asked.

"I hadn't looked that up yet." Callie flipped to the front of the report. "The police cleared her pretty quickly. She was barely a person of interest."

"That doesn't sit right with my stomach," Jag said. "Most people find their friend like that, they're not going to run away."

"Not everyone is cool under pressure."

"That's not being cool. That's being human," Jag said.

"Holy shit." Callie tapped her finger on the piece of paper. "Read that name out loud, because I think I'm seeing things."

"Carol Armstrong," Jag said. "Any relation to Leslie Armstrong?"

"I don't know. But you have quicker access to birth records and whatnot than I do," she said, twisting her body and handing him the laptop. She batted her eyelashes and tilted her head. "And while you're at it, find out where she might be now."

"As if you had to use that ploy to get me to find out that answer." He leaned over and smacked her lips with a wet kiss. "Give me a few minutes."

While he dug into Carol Armstrong and her life, she started making copies of important parts of different files. With different colored pencils, she made notes on each one, tacking them up on the board and drawing arrows to any potential connections they'd made between the victims.

Which were nearly none.

Only the Mood Ring Killer victims knew each other.

And two random victims of the Trinket Killer had a connection because they crossed paths working out at the same gym.

But one was killed holding a gold dolphin.

The other a silver one.

And they barely knew each other, just took the same spinning class on occasion.

But that meant the killer might have done the same.

"Motherfucker," Jag said. "Carol Armstrong is indeed the daughter of Leslie and John Armstrong. I'm shocked this didn't get red-flagged or that Albert or especially Ajax didn't know about it."

"Well, they might have a few years on you, but I'm not sure either of them were on the force that year. Albert might have been a senior in high school."

"True," Jag said. "Anyone ever tell you that you're always the smartest person in the room?"

She laughed. "You used to tell me the complete opposite."

"I was jealous."

"Of course. I'm awesome," she said. Her skin heated, and her heart swelled. It had been a long time since she felt this at ease with Jag. Actually, she wasn't sure discussing an investigation had ever been quite like this. "But that's because right now I'm working with the best."

"Oh, babe, flattery will so get you whatever you want tonight," he said with a wicked grin. "So, it looks like Leslie and John got a divorce when Carol was in grade school. The last known address for Carol Armstrong is college. She seems to disappear after that, and I can't find a marriage license. I do have a current address for her father, so let's pay him a visit tomorrow."

"As in us?"

"Absolutely. We'll do it right after I'm officially off duty."

"What if I do it while you're working?"

He stood, heaving her to his chest. He wrapped his arms around her waist, splaying his hands over the small of her back. "I don't want you going anywhere alone. I don't trust that this killer doesn't have a thing for you."

"You keep saying that, but other than my body type, which there are lots of women who—"

He hushed her with his mouth. "Last year, I tried to show you I loved you by being a Neanderthal and telling you what you can or can't do. I won't do that now, though I'm not going to give you his address."

She cocked her head. "That's pretty much telling me what to do."

"We both have learned to trust our gut instincts over the years. This killer has been waiting for something to happen to start killing again. Now, you had nothing to do with the start of the last cycle, but your sister finished it, and you showed up in

Seattle, and we have a dead body. And not on the mainland. On my island."

"You can stop now. I get it," she said as a chill climbed up her body. No matter how much she wanted to deny she couldn't have anything to do with what was happening, her conscience wouldn't allow it. Everything he said was spot-on. "I'll wait until you get off work."

"Thank you." He leaned in to kiss her, but she pulled back.

"Why are you doing all this? Sharing all this with me when we both know damn well you shouldn't be."

"If I tell you the truth, you have to promise you won't toss anything at me."

"I promise," she said with narrowed eyes. She couldn't imagine what he might say that would piss her off so much she'd want to cause him bodily harm.

Then again, he did have a way of finding her Achilles' heel and slicing through it with a razor-sharp knife.

"Because you're not going to report on it. You're not going to use it to get ratings. You're not going to go behind my back and use police information that we're keeping from the public to better your career."

For about five seconds, rage seared her heart. It burned through her bloodstream, reaching every part of her body, but it was quickly doused with a cold dose of reality.

Because he was right.

She'd been a ruthless reporter, willing to toss her own boyfriend under the bus if that meant getting the story first. She'd used him and the information he'd been kind enough to feed her during any investigation.

And all she'd done was shit on him.

"Oh, Jag, I'm so sorry."

He jerked his head back. "For what?"

"For being such a fucking bitch. You did so much for me, and I treated you like shit."

"Babe, we both made mistakes. But that was then, and this is now."

"You know, when you catch this bastard, I'm going to have to ask the publisher for an extension to rewrite the damn book."

"We could write it together," he whispered.

She swallowed, trying desperately to digest his response, but his lips came crashing down on hers. His tongue probed, finding every crevice inside her mouth, making it impossible for her to process the ramification of his words.

His hands found the back of her thighs, and he lifted her effortlessly off the floor, resting her ass on the desk.

All of a sudden she was painfully aware of her surroundings. She froze.

"What's wrong?"

"Not here."

He lifted her into his arms and pulled open the door. "Good call," he murmured against her ear. He dabbled her neck with kisses as he made his way up the stairs.

Once in his bedroom, it was a frenzy to remove their clothing. She couldn't get hers off fast enough. Her desire for him raced through her bloodstream like a freight train out of control. It was as if she were afraid she might not ever have him again, so she needed to make sure this time his passion would be burned inside her forever.

So she'd never forget him.

Ever.

Oh, God. She loved him so much that letting him go again would be damn near impossible.

They tumbled to the bed. His hands cupped her

breasts, pinching and twisting her nipples while he kissed her with intense greed.

She reached for him, but he kept batting her hand away, so she gave up and sank into the mattress, letting him have his way with her.

He knew her body better than she did. He teased her with his fingers and tongue, bringing her to the edge, letting her hang there for seconds before pulling back, only to start again. Only this time, he thrust into her hard and deep.

Digging her fingers into his back, she gasped. Her body jerked and shuddered. She couldn't catch her breath. She tried to fill her lungs, but all she managed to do was make herself dizzy.

She wrapped her arms and legs around him as tight as she could while he buried his face in her neck. Their bodies moved as one while their orgasms collided in a fiery ball and exploded between them, connecting them as one soul.

"I love you," he whispered.

A single tear rolled down her cheek. "I love you too," she said. "But it doesn't change anything."

14

Jag stared out at the water as the ferry made its way across Puget Sound from Whidbey Island to the mainland. He had spent most of the morning grappling with his feelings for Callie. She said the words. She might have tried to discount them, but she still let them come out of her mouth.

That was a start.

Of course, she'd said nothing about his thought on them co-writing the book, which had honestly come out of nowhere, but it made sense in a weird way. Hell, he'd already helped her rewrite a few chapters, and he'd worked a little bit on his chapter this morning before leaving for work. She seemed to like his suggestions. Well, most of them.

And she didn't argue with him on the few things

that he asked she remove, though she did ask for clarification.

While he hated dealing with the Trinket Killer again, he loved working with Callie.

Now he was going to spend the afternoon dealing with three dead bodies, bringing the count to five.

He pulled off the ferry and headed toward Carkeek Park where all three women had been found. The Trinket Killer had never gone on a mass killing before. Nor had she accelerated her murders like this. It had taken her six years to kill twelve people. And if she was responsible for the Mood Ring victims, six in a twelve-month period.

Those numbers churned up his heartburn. They could mean something. Then again, the Trinket Killer seemed to be acting erratically lately by not following her usual MO. There had to be a reason.

There was always a reason.

He pulled into the parking lot of the park where it was already a bustle of activity. His heartburn kicked up as he rolled past the Channel 5 news van and Bailey and her crew. He parked his vehicle near all the other police cars and made his way to the crime scene tape. He flashed his badge and signed the log before ducking under the tape and finding Albert.

"Hey, thanks for coming out," Albert said.

"Can't say I'm thrilled to have an invite to this party." Jag swallowed the bile bubbling up his esophagus. He took a deep cleansing breath, mentally prepping his mind for what he was about to see. For the last year, he'd lived a quiet life. No murders. No deadly crime that required him to harden his soul. Sure, there had been a deadly car crash on the island, which affected him just as deeply, but the emotions were different. "So, tell me why I'm here." Jag already knew the answer, but he wanted Albert to give him the rundown.

"We've got two prostitutes."

"The Trinket Killer never murdered a prostitute before," Jag said.

"Maybe not and as we've both said, this could be a copycat who doesn't know that or doesn't care, but we've got rose gold trinkets in their left hands. However, a big difference is the bodies were just dumped. Tossed into a shallow grave together. And they'd started to decompose, so they've most likely been here a few days."

"We still don't have an ID on the girl from the island," Jag said, rubbing his temples. The killer had burned off the victim's fingerprints, and so far, they couldn't match the victim to any missing persons. "Any idea who these girls are?"

"Yeah." Albert led Jag toward the shallow grave where the medical examiner was still working on the bodies while the CSI team set down numbers and took pictures of evidence. "Both had licenses on their persons. They were reported missing by a friend last week."

"Another sex worker?"

Albert nodded. "They use an adult chat room sometimes to meet clients. According to their friend, they were both to meet someone on that app the night they went missing."

"That's a bit of a coincidence." Jag eased down a slight incline, careful not to slip on the muddy hillside. The sound of a camera shutter echoed in his ears. The CSI team milled about, logging in evidence. The medical examiner knelt over the bodies.

"Hey, is that a wig?" Jag made his way to the head of one of the victims. A blond wig had been tossed to the side, exposing short red hair.

"I wonder if our killer knew or even cared."

"This doesn't feel right," Jag said with his hands on his hips. He glanced around the wooded area.

"The bodies aren't presented in the same way the others were."

"But we have rose gold raven trinkets in their hands, and we have this." Albert waved to one of the other detectives who strolled over and handed Albert a plastic bag with a note inside. "This is really why I wanted you out here now."

Jag took the bag into his hands and held it up high. It was a white piece of computer paper with bold words written in dark ink matching the last note that Callie had gotten. He drew it a little closer to his face and squinted.

Bringing me back has forced my hand. It's all your fault. Had you just let it go and let me stay away from Seattle, this would have never happened.

"What do you make of it?"

"I don't know," Jag said, scratching his head. "Mind if I take a picture of this?"

"I'm not showing this to the press, so I don't want it getting out."

"I'll just write the message versus the image," Jag said. "I have a feeling this is meant either for me or Callie, but I'm not understanding the concept of bringing me back. It makes it sound like the Trinket Killer left the area and came back. Which makes sense in a weird way since we had that fourteen-year gap between the mood rings and the dolphins. But other than Stephanie and Callie's ruthless coverage of the killer, I don't get the connection."

"I'm glad you said ruthless, because that's exactly what she was doing back then," Albert said. "She played a fine line between sensationalizing the killer and being a bitch to the cops all in the name of telling the public the truth, but she wasn't half as bad as Bailey. She's already going down the Trinket Killer road."

"With me here, she'll take that angle, I'm sure. I mean, why bring the Langley chief of police into the city of Seattle, unless it had to do with his one unsolved case."

Albert took the note and handed it back to his detective. "We can certainly connect the two bodies on Whidbey with these two, which officially gives us a serial killer. What I can't decide is if I want to acknowledge we believe the Trinket Killer is back or not."

"What happened with your other case?"

"Oh, we caught the guy, so that's closed," Albert said.

"All right. Do you want my opinion?"

"I do," Albert said. "Because if we announce

the Trinket Killer is back, that's going to create a shitstorm for both of us."

"Bring on the shitstorm," Jag said. "But I've got one more suggestion for you."

"Yeah, what's that?"

Jag glanced over his shoulder and stared at all the news crews setting up for a live feed for the evening news.

"Let me do it."

"Excuse me?"

"Let me make the announcement, and let me talk directly to the killer, calling her a she, and let's see what happens."

Albert pinched the bridge of his nose and let out a long breath. "Calling the killer a she is a big deal. The public will react to that, and so will the killer."

"I'm banking on that," Jag said. "I want the Trinket Killer to talk back to me, though it will probably be to Callie, so I was hoping she could at least be in the picture frame."

"That's dangerous," Albert said. "I doubt the commissioner will go for that."

"Ask him and then set up a press conference. I don't want her to say anything. I don't even want her front and center. I just want her present and visible."

"Why is this so important to you?" Albert asked.

"I don't think the killer has any faith in me to solve the case, but I think she believes Callie can. And I think the escalation in murders and that note are ways to scare Callie into leaving again."

Albert's eyebrows curved. "That's a bold theory."

"You don't buy it?"

"Actually, it sounds spot-on," Albert said. "I'll set it up."

"Let me know. I've got an errand to run, and I'll make sure Callie is on the next ferry to the mainland."

"Don't talk to the reporters on your way out."

Jag turned on his heel and headed toward the parking lot, waving his hand over his head. "No worries. Be safe, man."

No sooner did his feet land on pavement than Bailey and Jackie raced to his side, shoving a microphone in his face.

"Why were you called in?" Jackie asked.

"Is it because the Trinket Killer is back?" Bailey asked with a smug grin.

"No comment." Jag opened the patrol car door.

"We heard there were two murders on the island. Are they related?" Jackie asked.

"You ladies have a great evening." He turned the key and slammed the gearshift into reverse. He was going to hate having to face Bailey in a press conference. Once this was over, he was so going to enjoy going back to living his quiet life on the island.

Hopefully, with Callie.

Callie stood next to Jag, squeezing his hand as if she were falling off a ledge and he was her lifeline.

"Since when are you this nervous interviewing someone?" Jag asked.

She didn't get a chance to answer as the front door to John Armstrong's modest home in a suburb on the west side of Seattle swung open.

"Hello?" an older man with bright silver hair asked. He had a darker skin tone, as if he'd been lying in the sun for a few weeks. Deep wrinkles lined his lips and eyes. "May I help you?"

"We're sorry to bother you." She cleared her throat. "My name is Callie Dixon, and this is Langley Chief of Police Jagar Bowie."

"I know who he is," John said. "Did something happen?"

"I'm not here on official business," Jag added, holding his hand up.

"Then why are you here?" John asked.

"Long story short," Callie started. "I'm writing a book about the Trinket Killer and we—"

"I'm not giving you a statement about my ex-wife and whatever she might have done," John said.

"I don't want a statement." Callie flicked some of her long hair over her shoulder. "We'd like to ask you about your daughter and her college roommate," Callie said.

"Oh." John ran a hand over his face, pulling open the door. "Would you like to come in?"

"Thanks." Jag pressed his hand on the small of her back, nudging her forward. "We won't take up too much of your time. We were also hoping to get updated contact information for Carol."

"That I can't help you with." John led them to the family room where he took a seat in a recliner.

Callie made herself comfortable on the sofa, placing her elbow on the armrest while Jag continued to stand, stuffing his hands in his pockets and checking out the few pictures on the mantel.

"Why not?" Callie asked.

"I haven't spoken to my daughter since right after the murder of her roommate, and before that, we didn't have a good relationship. Her mother and I had a horrible marriage. Our divorce was even worse. Over the years, Leslie poisoned my daughter against me, and no matter what I did, Carol just didn't want anything to do with me." John shook his head. "And I didn't do much to get her back, and that's something I struggle with every day."

"You have no idea where she went?" Callie asked.

John shook his head. "When her mother committed suicide, I hired a private investigator to look for Carol, but he came up empty-handed. It's like she completely vanished." John glanced toward Jag. "You know, while I didn't like my ex-wife much, I have a hard time believing she killed herself. You knew her. Worked with her. What do you think?"

"I've wondered that myself," Jag said.

"She was accused of tampering with evidence on the Trinket Killer case. Did she do it?"

"I hate to admit it, but she did." Jag nodded. "I wish I knew why. It doesn't make sense that she'd do that with the Trinket Killer murders and no other case."

"I do know that Leslie loved her job. And from

what I remember, she was good at it. But as a wife, well, she was insanely jealous. I couldn't go out of the house without her thinking I was cheating on her. She used to wake Carol up in the middle of the night when I was working the C rotation."

"You're a fireman, right?" Callie asked.

"Retired. But yeah. Anyway. Leslie always thought I was cheating, and she told Carol that. Carol believed her, and when I met my second wife, things just got even worse. Truthfully, I was a selfish prick back then. If I knew I was never going to see my daughter again, I might have not gotten married so fast, but I can't change the past, can I?"

Jag held up a picture frame. "Is this your second wife and children?"

Callie stretched out her arm, wanting to take a close look at the new family.

"Yes. That's Tina, my wife. And we had twin boys, Jack and Billy. In that picture they had just graduated high school, but they are twenty-one now. They both joined the Navy," John said with a bright smile.

"Where's your wife now?" Callie asked, trying to keep her hands from shaking. His wife had beautiful long blond hair.

Styled just like Renee's and Stephanie's when they'd been murdered.

"She's visiting her mom. She's in a nursing home. I expect her back in about an hour," John said. "Why are you here?"

Jag sat on the edge of the sofa. "We are here in part because we're in the middle of an investigation that could be connected to the murder of your daughter's college roommate."

John let out a big puff of air. "I love my daughter. I really do. Not a day goes by that I don't think about her and wonder and worry about what she's doing, but she had a temper. She could be wickedly vicious."

"How so?" Jag asked.

"She had a razor-sharp tongue, for one. She had a way of cutting right through a person's heart. She knew how to hurt people. I could take it, but my wife, not so much, and once she gave birth to the twins, I had to really think about my boys. Not that Carol came to visit often, but I stopped letting her spend the night. That didn't go over well. She'd call here in the middle of the night, threatening to kill my wife and kids. She'd sometimes show up at two in the morning banging on the doors. It got so bad, I moved."

"Did you ever call the police?" Callie clutched the picture. Could this Carol person be their killer? Had it all started when her father remarried? But why kill the roommate? What had she done?

Callie's head throbbed. The pounding was deafening.

"No," John said with a deflated tone. "But by the time Carol went to college and I moved my family, things settled down."

"Did Carol ever hurt animals? Or get into physical fights with other people?" Jag asked.

"What are you getting at, son?" John sat up taller. "Do you think my daughter killed her roommate? Because she was cleared... oh, you think my ex-wife might have helped... oh my. You think my daughter is this Trinket Killer."

Damn. He put that together quickly.

"We don't think anything right now," Jag said. "But we do need to find her. Did Leslie stay close to her after the murder? Because to be honest, I had no idea she had a kid, and I worked with her for years."

"No. The murder changed their relationship as well. I really don't know what happened between them, but Carol left Seattle and told both of us we'd never see her again." John opened the drawer of the end table next to the recliner and pulled out a small pocket photo album. "Here are some pictures of her when she was a child. I don't have many and none after she turned thirteen, but maybe they can help you."

"Thanks. We really appreciate it." Callie took the booklet in her hands. "Any ideas on where she could have gone or any identities she might have taken on? Any little details you can think of might help us find her."

"I can't think of anything off the top of my head." John pulled out his wallet. "But here's the private investigator's card. I'll sign a waiver so he can give you whatever he's found. I would like to find her. She'd be forty-two now. I can't even fathom what she'd look like. I pass women on the streets with shoulder-length brown hair and brown eyes, and I wonder, could that be my Carol?" Tears welled in John's eyes. "I'm a good father, but I failed my only daughter."

Callie reached out and took John's hand. "I've made some pretty horrible mistakes during my lifetime, and last year my sister was murdered."

John gasped. "Oh my. I'm so sorry, dear."

"Thank you," Callie said. "I often feel as though I failed her. But I have to remind myself over and over again that hindsight is twenty-twenty, and even if I could go back in time, I wouldn't be going back with the knowledge I have today, so I'd probably play the same hand the same way."

John's lips curved into a small smile. "You're a wise young woman."

"That she is," Jag said. "Thank you so much for your time, sir."

"You're welcome. Thank you for your service, young man."

"You as well," Jag said.

"And please, if you find my Carol, will you let me know, even if it's bad news?" John stood, showing them to the door.

"We sure will." Callie felt compelled to give the man a hug. "Take care of yourself." Callie stepped outside. The sun had set, and a cool chill settled across her bones. She held up the pocket photo album, flipping to one of the last pages. She stared at an image that took her breath away. She clutched her heart and gasped.

"What is it?" Jag asked.

"That kind of looks like a young Kara."

15

Jag leaned against the kitchen counter at his parents' house, staring at the coffee machine, willing it to brew faster while his father stood in front of the toaster, tapping his fingers as if that would make the bagels jump up quicker.

"Where's Callie?" his father asked.

"In the shower," Jag said. "Thanks for letting us stay here tonight."

"Anytime. I just wish you didn't have to leave so early. Your mom would love to put on a big breakfast."

"I have to be at the office by eight." He poured two mugs of coffee and handed one to his father. "We're also putting some pieces of the puzzle together when it comes to the Trinket Killer."

"Well, that's good news," his father said. "It's good to have Callie back."

A smile tugged at Jag's lips. "I have to agree. But it could be short-lived."

"Are you saying that for my benefit or yours?"

"Probably both. I'm just trying to be realistic. I mean, I never expected that she'd return."

"But she did."

Jag blew on the hot liquid. "And so did the Trinket Killer."

"You really think that bastard is back?"

"You saw my press conference," Jag said. "She's back, and she's out for blood. I'm just not sure what her end game is, but we've got our first good solid lead, if we can find her."

"We? Who is this we you speak of?"

Jag laughed. "You and Mom think you're being so coy, but you're not. And yes, the we is me and Callie. We've always made a good team when I check my ego at the door and she's not in it for ratings."

His father rested a strong arm on his shoulder. "I'm proud of you, son."

"Thanks, Dad. I know I was a bit of an asshole for a while there."

"When you were forced to take a leave from the

police department and Callie left, you said and did a lot of things that hurt your mother."

"I know, and I've apologized profusely."

His father nodded. "It's water under the bridge. But we know you and understand you better than most. You've just gotten your life back in order, and if it were just Callie coming back into your life, I'd be biting my tongue, but adding in a killer that consumed you for the better part of four years and then nearly destroyed you last year, I find myself wanting to remind you of how dark things got for you."

"You don't have to." Jag tapped the center of his chest. "I haven't forgotten. But I am a different man than I was even six months ago. This isn't about having the best record in the department or making some crazy name for myself. It's about justice and doing my job. That's all I care about."

"And what about Callie? What does she care about these days?"

"Not ratings," Jag said with a chuckle. "But she's a little lost. She doesn't know what to do next. Once this book is done, she plans on leaving and heading to the East Coast to maybe write another true crime book, but I can tell she has no idea what she wants."

"Maybe that's because she's fighting what she's wanted and needed all along."

Jag laughed. "Sometimes I think this family has loved her more than I have."

His father raised his mug. "She's something special, and she brings out the best in you."

The toaster popped up a couple of bagels. His father went about slathering them with cream cheese. He set them on two plates and sat down at the kitchen table.

Jag joined him, snagging one of the crispy raisin bagels covered with melting cream cheese. He dipped his index finger in the creamy white stuff, sucking it into his mouth before taking a big bite. He chewed as fast as he could and swallowed. "I want to ask her to stay."

"So do it."

"I want to give her the engagement ring back."

His father spit out his coffee. "As in you still want to marry her? Like jump right back into that pool?"

"I take it you think that idea is crazy."

"No, son. I don't think it's nuts. Not from your perspective. But from hers? It might be." His father ripped off a piece of his bagel and plopped it in his mouth. "Why did she come back?"

"To try to get an interview from me and finish her book," Jag said. His heart skipped a beat as he realized she never really gave him a second thought. Being with him during these last two weeks hadn't been something she'd thought about like he had over the last year.

Or if she had, she hadn't let him know that.

"That's the only reason?" his father asked.

"That's what she told me."

"And you took that at face value?"

"Dad, what are you getting at?" Jag asked.

"She was madly in love with you. She knew things about you and that case that no one else did. She could have written that chapter about you without ever interviewing you. Did you ever consider that maybe, even if it was subconscious, that she came back because she wanted and needed to be with you?"

"No, actually, I hadn't," Jag admitted. Not for one second did he ever consider Callie came back for the sole purpose of being with him. Nope. It had been about the book.

Which meant she hadn't really changed.

Only she had.

Jag rubbed his temples. "She keeps telling me she's leaving soon."

"Do you believe her?"

"Of course. Why wouldn't I?"

"Have you ever thought that she's wanting you to fight for her? Because, no offense, son, but you never did that before."

Jag stuffed another large bite of his bagel in his mouth. He chewed slowly, taking in some coffee, letting it soak the bread as he stared out the window into the dark morning sky. His father was right. He didn't fight for her a year ago because she'd bruised his fragile ego. "I've told her I still love her."

"And what does she say?"

"That she loves me too, but she can't go back. That once this book is done, she's closing the chapter and moving on."

"And what do you think that looks like?"

"Dad, pardon my language, but I have no fucking clue. I didn't think I'd ever have a second chance, so I'm grasping at a lot of straws here. I'm doing everything I can think of to show her how much I respect her, value her, and love her. Outside of that, I'm at a total loss."

His father chuckled. He pushed his empty plate away and took a good gulp of his coffee. "I'm not sure you can do much more than that, but I want you to consider one thing."

"Yeah. What's that?"

"Look closely at what is making things so different right now from where you were a year ago."

"That's actually easy. I'm not the lead detective, and she's not a reporter."

"Okay. That's one aspect. But dig deeper, because it's more than that. Your old jobs are too superficial and an external conflict that is easily resolved. The two of you are on a different level, and I think it's more about understanding and knowing what you want out of life. You used to think all that mattered was your record, but now you know that serving your community is what it's all about. You know that being a police officer isn't about the impeccable record but about doing right by the people you serve. How is what she's doing different than being a reporter? What is the purpose of her writing this book?"

Wow. That was a really good question and one that Jag had spent a lot of time pondering, but not one he was willing to ask Callie. Not yet, anyway. "Honestly, I think it's threefold."

"Explain," his father said.

"She's doing it for Stephanie. To keep her memory alive as well as every other victim. To give them a voice and make sure their stories are heard."

"That's a noble cause," his father said. "What else?"

"To change the direction of her original reporting. Make up for the sensationalism and go back to what made her want to become an investigative reporter to begin with."

"And could the third aspect of this possibly be to reconnect with you and see where that takes the both of you?" his father asked.

That wasn't where Jag planned on taking the third part of his thought process, but it made more sense than his theory, which had been… Well, fuck, he didn't have a third tier.

"It could be," Jag agreed. "But she's constantly telling me she's leaving. Like last night when Mom said we could stay in the same room, Callie made a point of letting me know that it was no big deal if we didn't share a bed because when the book was done, she was gone."

"But you two slept together anyway."

Jag nodded. "Why dirty two sets of sheets for Mom to clean."

"You are my son." His father let out a short laugh and quickly cleared his throat. "But it sounds like she might be trying to convince herself that she should leave and perhaps subconsciously wanting you to ask her to stay. But giving her the ring and re-proposing marriage might be a little rushed and could scare her away."

"What do you suggest I do?"

"I take it she doesn't know you found the ring?" his father asked.

He shook his head.

"Show her that you painstakingly took the time to find it and keep it so that she knows you wanted her to come back to you. Just because you still love each other and are compatible in bed, that doesn't equal forever." His father reached across the table and tapped his finger against Jag's chest. "Letting her see and feel what you've been hoping for all this time will let her know that your life has stalled without her in it, and maybe she'll be able to see that she came back for one reason only."

Jag waited for a long minute for his father to tell him what that reason was, but his father just sat there and stared at him. Jag let out a long breath. "Are you going to clue me in to why she really came back to Seattle?"

"You really need someone to fill in the blank, son?"

Jag sipped his coffee. His pulse pounded in his head. "I hope you're right, Dad, because I'm going to lay my heart out on the table for her to destroy."

"I think she might surprise you."

"I hope you're right, because I don't think I could get over her again."

"Son, you never got over her the first time."

Callie tossed her purse on the kitchen table in Jag's house. If she'd gotten three hours of sleep last night, it would have been a miracle.

"Are you going to be okay?" Jag asked, smoothing her hair from her face.

She sighed. "I'll be pacing until I get the yearbooks from Carol Armstrong's college." Callie rested her head on Jag's shoulder, wrapping her arms around his strong frame. "I feel sick to my stomach about digging into Kara's background, but I'm shocked about how little I know about her."

"We looked at their relationship, how they interacted with their friends, which was hard since they'd just moved to Seattle from Colorado. Once Kara was cleared, there was no reason to dig any deeper."

She lifted her head. "Jag, I should know more. She worked with me on this book. Hell, she worked with me on the side during the investigation of the Trinket Killer. I trusted her."

"So did I," Jag said.

Callie shook her head. "I told her things I shouldn't have. Things you told me about the investigation that I swore I'd keep to myself. She helped me form the theory about Adam Wanton. She all but talked me into going after him in the press, which made you look like an idiot."

Jag pressed his warm, tender lips on her forehead. "Let's first find out if Kara is indeed Carol. That shouldn't be too hard to figure out."

"God, if she is, I've been such a fool, and so many people died because of me." She squeezed her eyes so tight, pushing out a few tears.

"Babe, look at me."

"What?" She tilted her head, blinking wildly.

"I'm the king of self-blame for all these deaths, especially Stephanie's. If what you and I are thinking, and the Trinket Killer has been right under our noses for the last few years, then I'm going to have to brace for impact because we both know people like Bailey are going to make me look like an incompetent idiot. And maybe I was. But this killer is smart, smarter than us; you even said so in your book. And if Kara is the killer, she had her mother's help. Think about that for a second."

"Trust me, I've been thinking about it. But there are still a few things that don't add up." Her mind splintered off into a million directions, firing thousands of questions and scenarios, but none totally made sense. There were too many unknown factors.

And she still didn't want to believe that Kara could have been lying to her for a good three years.

"Will you go through a couple things with me before you head to the office?"

He glanced at his watch. "I have twenty minutes."

"You were a beat cop when Renee was murdered," Callie said.

"I took the call. My partner and I were the first on the scene." Jag took a step back and fiddled with the Keurig, shoving his travel mug under the spout. "The lead detective retired three months later, but it had already gone cold. It wasn't until we had a fourth murder, which was my first case, that we put it together."

"And that's when I gave the killer a name, and shortly after I did that, I got an email from Kara."

"Okay," Jag said, taking a second mug and

pressing the start button on the coffee machine. "Do you have all that correspondence?"

"I do."

"Will you email it to me?"

"Of course," she said. "For about a year, I kept her at arm's length in the sense that I interviewed her and took as much information as I thought was useful, but I was more interested in finding the killer and getting ratings."

"But you did a personal story about her and Renee."

"I did. It was a filler piece, but it was what started our friendship. Kara seemed generally interested in the investigation. She started picking up patterns... Fuck, she was planting those things at the crime scene and in my head."

"We don't know that."

Callie snagged the cup of coffee he handed her. "Don't coddle me or try to make me feel better. We need to be realistic and keep our heads in the game."

"I am. We don't know anything for sure. We first need to find out who and where Carol is. We do that, we make a plan."

"Wow. You really have changed," she said. "I like this new, calm, levelheaded man."

"Like? What about love? I prefer that word."

"Jag. Why do you have to do that? You know how I feel, but that doesn't change the fact that I'm still leaving."

"I don't want you to leave. I want you to give us a second chance. A real opportunity to see who we are now and where this might take us."

"I can't."

"Why not?" he asked. "Because I think we're worth taking a risk for." He took her by the hand and tugged her upstairs.

"We don't have time for sex."

He laughed. "I'm a guy. I can be done in a couple of minutes if I need to, but no, as much as I would love to have sex with you right now, that's not what I need to show you. Sit." He pointed to the bed.

"I'd rather stand." She folded her arms across her middle and stared at him. "What's this all about?"

He pulled open the top dresser drawer and took something out. He held a box in his hand.

"Oh, my God." She went to sit on the edge of the bed but missed, landing her ass on the floor with a thud.

He raced to her side, helping her up. "Are you okay?"

"No," she said. "Is that what I think it is?" She pointed to the jewelry box with a shaky finger. Her heart pounded in her chest so fast she thought it might explode.

"It's your engagement ring," he said, flipping open the box.

She gasped, covering her mouth. The half carat white diamond sparkled as if it had just been cleaned. It sat high in a six-prong silver setting. "I tossed that in a big pile of watery mud. How did you find it?"

"It took me three days of digging and sifting, but I got lucky."

"You sure did," she said, reaching out to touch it, but she snapped her hand back. "I can't believe you found it, much less kept it." She glanced up at him with tears burning in her eyes. "Why didn't you sell it?"

"If I did that, it would mean I had let you go, and I couldn't do that. I know I was an asshole at Ajax's party, but I was protecting my heart. I can't do that anymore. My heart wants what it wants, and it wants you. I love you. I always have, Callie. From the day you walked into that bar and challenged me to an intellectual debate. You make me want to be a better man."

She covered his mouth with her hand. "Stop talking." A wave of dizziness washed over her system. The room spun. She felt as though she might be sick. Taking in a few deep calming breaths, she battled the nausea, shoving it out of her mind. "You sound like you might propose again, and I don't want to have to turn you down."

He chuckled. "I'm not asking you to marry me. I know it's too soon for that. All I'm asking is for you to consider staying in Langley for three months after we catch this killer. If after that time you really don't think we are perfect for each other, then I'll take this ring and sell it. But if you do realize we should be together, then this ring goes back on your finger."

Well, that was a lot to digest in one morning. She blew out a puff of air. Three months. She could do three months. "Are you expecting me to live with you?"

"That's up to you," he said. "I certainly wouldn't say no to the prospect, but if you're not comfortable with that, I'd be happy just to have you on the island dating me, officially, with the world knowing. No secrets."

She laughed. "Yeah. That kind of fucked us the first time."

"Is that a yes?"

"I think I've utterly lost my mind, but yes." She pressed her hand on his chest when he moved in for a kiss. "However, as much as I love the view here, I'm not going to live with you."

Jag smiled like a teenage boy who just saw a naked girl for the very first time. "I'll take it."

She jumped to her feet. "Now get the fuck to work so I can do a deep dive into research."

"Lock the doors behind me and don't you dare leave this house." He kissed her nose. "And promise me you won't talk to Kara."

"I won't promise that," she said. "But I will let you know if I do."

"I guess I have to live with that."

She followed Jag to the front door, giving him a proper kiss before making sure everything was locked up tight. She shivered when she walked into Jag's home office. All the victims stared at her as if they were begging her to bring their killer to justice.

Flipping open her laptop, she made herself comfortable behind the desk. She pulled out a notebook and started organizing her thoughts, pushing the tiny excitement about her decision to stay for a while to the back of her brain.

Every ten or fifteen minutes she'd check her emails to see if any of her requests had come through. Nothing yet. Meanwhile, she did her own searches, and one of them consisted of looking up the dead college roommate.

But so far, Callie had found nothing other than what had been reported.

Jag had promised if Albert or the cold case detective found anything, he'd let her know, but so far, she hadn't heard from Jag either, and it had been over an hour since he'd gone to work.

Well, that wasn't too long.

She'd never been the most patient person, and today it was being tested to the limit.

Her email dinged, and a message from the college came through with an attachment. Butterflies filled her gut as she clicked the icon.

She scrolled through the digital yearbook until she found Carol Armstrong. She found seven different images, all equally disturbing because of the uncanny similarities.

"Oh, my God." Callie expanded one of the images with Carol and her roommate in an intimate embrace. Their arms wrapped around each other,

Carol had her lips smacked on her roommate's cheek. It could be seen as close friends, but Callie's gut told her it was more than that.

Callie pulled up another picture and studied Carol's features. She had long blond hair. Kara had short light-brown hair. They both had stunning blue eyes. Both had slender builds, though Kara was a tad bit more muscular. But what really freaked Callie out was the tattoo that dotted Carol's midriff. It was in the exact location as a blotchy mark that Kara always said was a birthmark.

But maybe it was a tattoo that she tried to remove.

Callie forwarded the information on to Jag, along with her thoughts about Carol having a relationship with her roommate. She pulled up police reports from the murder, and not a single person mentioned a potential love affair.

So, why did Carol kill women who also looked like her and her stepmother? Wait. In Carol's picture that her father had given them she had dark hair. And it wasn't as long. Not to mention she wore less makeup and wasn't as glitzy as the Carol at college.

No. Carol as a teenager was more like the Kara that Callie knew. Down-to-earth and very little maintenance. But Kara had a type. She liked her women to be girly-girls.

Ivy was a blond. With long hair, though she didn't style it the way… Fuck. It didn't matter because the killer styled some victims the way she wanted.

"Oh no," Callie whispered. Ivy could be next.

But the other thing that bothered her was Carol's stepmother, Tina. She looked young. Really young.

Callie tapped her cell, pulling up Jag's number. "Pick up," she whispered.

"Hey, babe," he answered on the second ring. "Everything okay?"

"Yes, I'm fine. But no. Things are not okay. I think I have something," she said.

"I just got your email, but I'm out of the office and hard to see much on my cell."

"Just more evidence that points to Carol and Kara being the same person, but I have another hunch."

"Lay it on me," Jag said.

"Didn't you think Tina looked young?"

"I'd say she was a trophy wife, why?"

"Would you say she could be close to Kara's age, which is forty-two?" Callie said as she tried to swallow, but her pounding heart lurching up to her throat made it impossible.

"That would make her a really young mom."

"But it's possible," Callie said. "What if Carol, Kara, or whoever the fuck we're dealing with knew Tina first. Introduced her to her father and then boom, no more friend or lover, and Carol goes off the deep end and starts killing people who look like her stepmother."

"That's an interesting theory," Jag said.

"I want to go talk with the stepmother."

"No. No. No," Jag said. "I don't want you leaving my house, much less the island."

She was about to say that Kara wasn't even here, but if she was the killer, she certainly was close, and maybe watching.

Jag had a point. But she couldn't sit idle.

"What if I could get Tina to come to me?"

"I could live with that, but how are you going to get her to come out to the island?"

"You forget, I used to be a manipulative reporter who was used to getting whatever I wanted."

"Oh, dear Lord, I'm terrified," he said with a laugh. "Do me a favor; let me know when and where so I can have someone watching, promise?"

"Absolutely. Thanks, Jag."

"For what?"

"For believing in me."

"What are good boyfriends for?"

"Christ, did I really just agree to be your girlfriend?" she asked, tongue-in-cheek. "Don't answer that. I'll talk to you later."

"Love you, babe."

"Right back at you."

16

"You've got to be fucking kidding me." Jag slammed his fist down on the steering wheel as he swerved his patrol car to the side of the road.

"I'm sorry," Albert said. "I wish it wasn't true."

"You're sure it was Ivy Thompkins body we found in Beverly Beach."

"All the medical records prove it," Albert said. "And the medical examiner pins the time of death at three in the morning the night of Ajax's party."

"Callie and Kara blew into town the day before."

"And supposedly Kara rolled right out of town the next day," Albert said. "When was the last time Callie saw either of them?"

"We both saw Kara the day the Trinket Killer

left a note for Callie at the Langley Inn, but I only got a glimpse of Kara the night of the party, and I believe that was the last time she's seen Ivy, but she's spoken to Kara on the phone numerous times."

"But not Ivy," Albert interjected.

"Seeing as though she's dead, no. It's always just been Kara or Carol."

"Yeah. Armstrong. That's a fucking blow, man. If what you and Callie are saying is true, Armstrong has been covering for her daughter for years."

"I'm thinking you might want to have someone take a closer look at her suicide." Jag glanced in his rearview mirror as a four-door sedan came barreling down the road.

"Already on it."

"Fuck. I've got to go. Some asshole is doing like eighty in a forty and coming up on a school zone."

"One more thing you need to know."

Jag kept his gaze on the approaching vehicle that didn't bother to slow down, even when Jag hit his siren and flashed his lights. "What's that?"

"We got a call from John Armstrong last night. His wife didn't come home. I pushed the missing person through even though it hasn't been twenty-four hours. I've put out a person of interest bulletin for Kara, and I've contacted the locals in the town you mentioned she and Ivy were supposed to be staying at, just to see if they even went there at all, but I'm sure it's a dead end."

"Well, we have to cover our bases." Jag gripped the steering wheel, ready to punch the gas. He'd call Callie after he dealt with this motherfucker.

At least he didn't have to worry about Callie leaving the house and meeting with Tina anymore.

Nope. He just had to worry about fucking Kara walking onto his island, if she wasn't already there.

"Can you order a checkpoint at the ferry?"

"Done," Albert said.

"All right. Stay in touch." Jag tapped his cell and peeled out onto the street in hot pursuit. He lifted the mic. "Isabelle, this is the chief. I'm pulling over a light-blue Sonata for doing eighty in a forty. Washington plates of ERI 778. Can you run them for me?"

"Jesus, that's fast."

"No shit, and he's about to enter a school zone. Find out where Jenna is. If he doesn't slow down, I'm taking his license on the spot."

"She's right here. Want me to send her out?"

"Yeah. I'm right by the elementary school." He hit his sirens so anyone near the school would hear him. Unfortunately, he felt the need to slow down since he was approaching ninety miles an hour. He sure as hell didn't want to cause harm to anyone, but he had to stop this asshole. "He flew by it, and I'm about to. She might be able to cut him off if she comes at it from the other side."

"She's already out the door."

The blue car disappeared around a sharp bend. Jag considered himself an excellent driver, but he wasn't a race car driver, so he slowed a little more as he took the curve as tight as he could.

"Fuck." He hit the brake and swerved, trying to avoid the vehicle he'd been chasing sitting right in the middle of the damn street. "Oh shit." As he turned hard right, his left tires lifted off the pavement. Before he knew it, his patrol car did a full three-sixty in the air, landing on its wheels before flipping one more time to the side.

His body jerked left and right. The airbag smashed into his face, snapping his neck back. He groaned as the car slowly came to a halt. He hung sideways, the seat belt keeping him still. Carefully, he undid the strap and climbed out of his car, then fell to his knees with every muscle in his body aching. His face felt like it had been used as a punching bag. The sun chose that precise moment to peek out from behind a cloud, forcing him to squint. A silhouette approached him carrying some kind of long stick or maybe a bat. He covered his eyes with his hand. "Kara?"

"Hello, Jag," Kara said, taking the bat and smacking it against her hand. "Sorry to have to do this." She raised the object high over her head.

Jag blinked as he tried to stand, but before he could catch his balance, a sharp pain vibrated against his head. He slumped to the ground, landing face-first on the pavement. His vision blurred. All he could hear was a loud ringing between his ears before a vast darkness overtook him.

Callie paced in front of the seafood diner on the docks in the center of downtown Langley. She'd left two messages on Tina's phone, but Tina would only text.

That was weird, but when pressed, Tina said it was because she didn't want her husband to know she was meeting with Callie.

Fine.

But why not call her now that she should be disembarking from the ferry?

Callie sat on the bench and glanced down the street. No sign of a police vehicle, but that didn't mean Jag didn't have eyes on her.

Callie: *Where are you? Tina should be here in twenty.*
Jag: *I'm ten minutes out. Don't worry.*

Right. Easier said than done. Only, she had no idea why she was so frazzled. It was just an interview. It wasn't like she was having lunch with Kara and confronting her about her identity.

But something felt off.

The sound of someone scuffing their feet behind her and the smell of fresh fried clams caught her attention. She stiffened her spine and slowly turned her head.

"Hi, Callie girl."

"Kara? What are you doing here?" Callie asked, trying to act all casual as if she wasn't terrified for her life.

At least Jag was on his way.

"I thought you and Ivy were in Oregon." Callie took the clam roll Kara offered. "Where's Ivy?"

"She's not here," Kara said. "Why don't we go for a walk? I think we have a lot to talk about."

"I can't. I'm meeting someone. An interview for the book. It's coming along really well. I think you'd like it." Callie said the words so fast she thought she might trip over them.

"We both know who you're meeting," Kara said. "And I'm here to tell you that Tina won't be showing up."

"Excuse me?" Callie swallowed.

Hard.

Her pulse raced. Her palms turned sweaty as she fumbled with her cell, trying to call Jag. She managed to hit the right button.

It rang.

And so did Kara.

Kara pulled out Jag's phone. "He's not coming either."

Callie dropped the clam roll to the ground. She slumped over. "Where is he? What did you do to him?"

"If you're asking if I killed him, the answer is no. Not yet. Now pick up the mess you made, and let's get out of here."

"I'm not going anywhere with you. I know who you are."

Kara laughed. "So, you think you have it all figured out, don't you?"

Callie didn't have a fucking clue, other than Kara and Carol were one in the same and her life as well as Jag's were hanging in the balance. "Why don't you fill in the blanks for me."

"I plan on it. But not here. I want Jag to hear this too."

"Why?"

Kara shrugged. "Because the only way I'm going to get away with this is if the two of you die together."

Jag blinked open his eyes. His head felt like someone hit him with a baseball bat.

Oh, wait. Kara had done just that.

He waited a few moments while his vision came into focus before trying to move off the cold, hard floor. His hands were bound behind his back, and his ankles were held together with duct tape. He managed to push himself to a sitting position using the wall. There were two boarded-up windows on the opposite side.

Someone groaned.

He glanced to his left, his heartbeat raging out of control. He let out a sigh of relief when he realized it wasn't Callie.

But it didn't last very long knowing she was out

there, all alone, waiting for Tina, who was lying on the ground with a nasty head wound.

Hopefully, Jenna had done exactly what he'd instructed, and the cavalry would be arriving shortly.

He scooted across the floor. "Are you okay?" he whispered.

Tina opened her eyes. "Who are you?"

"I'm Jagar Bowie, the chief of police for the city of Langley."

"You're the man who stopped by my house," she said.

He did his best to help her to a sitting position. She was bound the same as he was, but since Kara neglected to tie them to anything, he should be able to get them both out. He just had to do that before Kara came back.

And before she got ahold of Callie.

"I am, and my girlfriend, Callie Dixon, was going to try to set up a meeting with you today to discuss your stepdaughter." Jag pushed his back up against Tina's and started fiddling with the tape that bound her wrists. He had to be patient and methodical.

The latter he could handle.

The former still took a lot of practice.

"I know. I got her message. I was about to call her back when Kara showed up."

Jag paused. "You know her by that name. How is that possible?"

Tina let out a long breath. "When she moved back here with Renee, I ran into her."

"And you didn't tell your husband?"

"No." Tina slumped. "This is all my fault," she said with a tremor in her voice. She sniffled.

"Why do you say that?" He managed to fold back a piece of tape from her binding. His pulse increased. He should be able to have her hands freed in a few minutes. Hopefully that would give them enough time. Of course, he had no idea where they were. Or how long he'd been knocked unconscious.

"My husband is going to kill me," Tina mumbled.

Jag twisted his body, tugging at the tape, trying to unravel it. "I'm sure all he's going to care about is that you're safe. And I just want to help both of us get out of here. But I suspect Kara is going to go after my girlfriend, and I need to stop her. I think you might have some information that can help me."

"I first met Kara when I was an RA in her

dorm. She was a freshman, and I was getting my master's degree. We had a short affair right before I met her father. When I broke it off and told her about her dad, she didn't seem to care. I married her dad and had the twins and Kara went nuts. I couldn't tell her dad about the affair nor could I tell him that I thought she might have killed her roommate, but she was cleared. I always wondered, but I figured the police knew what they were doing."

"We do, but sometimes we get it wrong," Jag said. "And Kara had some help from her mother."

"That poor woman," Tina said between sobs. Her shoulders shook up and down, making it harder for Jag to deal with releasing her hands, but he wasn't going to say anything.

The woman needed to cry.

"What happened when you saw her and Renee?" Jag asked.

"At first, she tried to pretend she didn't know who I was. I let it go. I figured it was for the best. But then she reached out to me. I wanted to talk to her. I wanted to see if she was willing to talk to her father. He missed her so much and felt so guilty."

Finally, he'd pulled off the last piece of tape from her wrists. He held out his hands in front of her, and she immediately went to work.

"I take it she wasn't willing to reconcile," he said.

"Not with her father, no. But I made a huge mistake, and I had an affair with her for three months. I called it off about two weeks before her wife was murdered."

"Jesus," Jag muttered as he shook out his hands and went about releasing his legs as well as Tina's. "Did you ever think she might have killed her wife?"

"Honestly, the thought crossed my mind, but I was selfish. I wanted her out of my life and was willing to do whatever it took, but she let me go. Just told me to go back to her father and forget all about her. She told me she was fine. When Renee was murdered, I thought about reaching out, but I never did, and she never contacted me, so I went on with my life."

"Did you ever follow the Trinket Killer murders?" Jag asked.

"Not really. But a couple of the murders, my husband made the comment that the victims looked like me. He worried about me wandering around the city by myself, so I didn't."

Jag managed to push to his shaky feet. His head

throbbed. His stomach churned. He outstretched his arm, helping Tina.

"She's the killer, isn't she?"

"I believe so," Jag admitted.

"What have I done?" Tina cupped her face and shook her head. "I was so scared she'd hurt me or my boys or ruin my marriage. She can be so intoxicating, and I let that control me even though I knew deep down what I was doing was wrong."

"Don't beat yourself up over this. Kara worked with my girlfriend for years. I was one of the officers who ruled her out as a suspect. She had everyone snowed. None of this is your fault."

"I wish I could believe that, but I think deep down I've always known Kara wasn't quite right in the head, but she can be so charismatic."

Jag would have to agree. Kara was intelligent and carried herself with a sense of humble confidence. She never got in your face, but she always spoke her mind, and she always had facts to back it up. She had a way of making everyone around her feel comfortable.

But she also had an edge. One he'd seen a few times but ignored because she was, well, Kara.

"I understand," he said. "But for now, we need

to focus on how to get out of here. Do you have any idea where we are?"

Tina shook her head.

He made his way to the door. He twisted the handle. Locked. Of course. He patted his pants. No phone. No gun. No mic to call dispatch. He literally had no lifeline.

But he trusted his team.

He took a step back and kicked the door.

Nothing.

He did it again.

Still nothing.

He went over to the boarded-up window and kicked at that, and he made more headway as the wood cracked. He kept kicking, and Tina joined in until the wood splintered, opening a hole and letting the sun seep in.

"Well, it's still daytime," he said.

"Is that supposed to make me feel better?"

"Actually, yes," he said as he stepped through the open space. He took her hand and helped her. Scanning the area, he got his bearings. "Okay. It looks like we're not far from Pen Cove Park. You were supposed to meet with Callie at three, right?"

"Correct," Tina said.

He glanced to the sky. "It's just after three. I bet

that…" The sound of a vehicle approaching caught his attention.

"Oh, my God. That's her car."

He recognized the light-blue vehicle that raced by him earlier. "Come on." He took her by the hand and raced toward the back of the house. "You don't have a phone on you, do you?"

"No," Tina said.

Fucking wonderful. He was going to have to find a perfect stranger to help, but first, he needed to find a way to get Tina out of harm's way. "I want you to run to the park. Don't look back. Just keep on running until you find someone and call 9-1-1. Tell them that the Langley chief of police and Callie Dixon have been taken hostage by the Trinket Killer. Go." He shoved her. Hard.

She fumbled forward. Glancing over her shoulder she stared at him with wide eyes.

"Just do it. She can only go after one of us, and she's going to try to take me out first. Go."

Tina nodded and took off running.

Now all he had to do was stall and hope to fucking God he and Callie didn't end up dead.

17

Callie did her best to control her breathing and her panic. She pushed aside all negative thoughts about how she should have seen that Kara was the killer. It ripped her heart into a million pieces that she not only hadn't a clue, but that she'd spent the last year crying on her shoulder over Jag and over her sister.

"Stephanie," she whispered as she stared out the window, her hands bound together with duct tape. "Why did you have to kill my sister?"

"Such a complicated question." Kara took a turn down a side road heading toward one of the parks on the north end of the island.

"She knew you were the Trinket Killer?"

"No. She hadn't quite figured that out yet. But

she would have considering she had found out I was really Carol Armstrong."

"How'd that happen?" Callie took a slow breath, expanding her chest slowly. All she had to do was treat this like any other conversation. Kara liked to talk. She liked to express her opinion, and she always had one.

"Remember when Stephanie came to you and said she was seeing someone?"

Callie nodded.

"I was that someone. And I want you to know that I really cared about your sister. I really did. I never wanted to hurt her."

"Is that why you smashed her face in?" Bile smacked the back of Callie's throat. Her stomach churned.

Kara reached out, smacking Callie across the cheek.

Callie's head snapped, crash-landing against the window with a thud. She groaned. Probably not a good idea to fire back with sarcasm. Duly noted.

"Don't make me do that again," Kara said.

Callie lifted her bound hands and rubbed the side of her face. "Okay. So how did my sister find out your identity?" she asked as calmly as possible.

"She found an old picture that I kept. And in

true Stephanie form, she confronted me on it, and she didn't let up. Nope. She had to turn into a little Nancy Fucking Drew like you. If she told you who I was, you and that idiot boyfriend of yours would have figured it out." Kara glanced in Callie's direction. "Why the fuck did we have to come back here? Why did you make me do this all over again? It's your fault. Just like it was Renee's. If I had never come back to this godforsaken place, I could have tamed the beast."

That circled Callie back to an onslaught of other questions she needed answered. She clutched her chest. Images of her and her sister bombarded her mind. But it was her sister's voice tickling her ear, telling her to find out everything so that no victim would die in vain.

"What does that mean?" Callie asked.

"Wow. You really are a dumb fuck." Kara pulled into a side street that looped toward the water. She stopped in front of a boarded-up small house. Or maybe a shed. "It's amazing you and Jag got anywhere without me."

Callie glanced to the left. "That's funny because looking back, once you entered the picture, you directed my reporting. It was subtle, but I can see how as soon as I started opening up, you just twisted it, and I let you, and I, in turn, used it on Jag. You even went as far as to use your own mother to plant evidence and change the DNA samples so that Jag would catch Adam. Why'd you do that?"

Kara rammed the gearshift into park. "Because I planned on leaving Seattle with Stephanie. If we had a killer wrapped up nice and neat, it would be easy to leave, especially for her since she worried so much about you. But no, she had to go find my secret, and then my stupid bitch mother had to gain a conscience and mislabel one of the samples on purpose. She wanted to get caught, but before she could confess what she'd done and rat me out, I—"

"You killed her."

"Well, would you look at that, Callie girl grew a fucking brain."

Callie let out a dry laugh. "And you killed Adam Wanton."

"Of course I did. I needed him to disappear so people might still believe he was the killer even if my mom fucked all that up and your stupid boyfriend jumped the gun on the arrest." Kara reached over and opened the vehicle door. "Get out."

On wobbly legs, Callie stepped from the car. She scanned the area but wasn't exactly sure where she was. She and Jag had spent some time on the island when they'd been dating, but they always liked Fort Casey over any other place. "Why'd you kill your college roommate?" She needed to focus on the patterns and motives of the murders. The psychology behind it. She had to understand more about how Kara thought and felt about her actions if she was going to figure out how to get out of this situation alive.

And if she wound up dead.

At least she'd know the truth before she went six feet under.

Someone had to.

"She wasn't Tina."

"Your stepmother," Callie said matter-of-factly. "Why the mood ring?"

"Because that's the very first gift that Tina ever bought me. I was shocked when she didn't tell the cops that. It was the first moment I knew I could get away with it. Not that I thought I wanted to at the time." Kara shoved Callie against the hood of the sedan before reaching in and opening the glove box. She pulled out a gun before leaning against the car. She folded her one hand across her middle but made sure the other one pointed the weapon right at Callie. "I was sick to my stomach for days over what I had done. It was like an out-of-body experience. I was bending over the body, pounding her face with some snow globe or something when I realized what I'd done. I quickly got up, cleaned off all the blood, changed my clothes, and ran off down the hallway screaming like a madwoman."

"But you killed again. And all women who looked like Tina."

Kara nodded. "We all have a type. I like women with long blond hair who are tall and slender and smart. That often gets me in trouble. I can't tell you how many women I have dated that I've had to kill because they figure it out."

Callie swallowed. "But you don't just kill gays."

"Nope. Sometimes I kill because I have to. I kill friends or colleagues or hookers because I get the hankering."

"But you had a fourteen-year gap when you left Seattle."

Kara shook her head. "Actually, I didn't. When I left here the first time, I went to Vermont, and I met a lovely woman by the name of Heidi. We were madly in love, until she decided the fun was over. She thought I stifled her. That I was too jealous of her other friends."

"So you killed her." Callie let out an exasperated sigh. "How many women did you kill in Vermont?"

"Only six. And since I know what the next question is, I'll answer it for you. I left them all with a pillow."

"A pillow?" Callie snapped her gaze in Kara's direction and stared at her with wide eyes. "In their hand?"

"No. Under their head."

"Why that object?"

"Again, it had to do with gifts between me and my lover. See, Renee, she loved dolphins. And Ivy, ravens. Yes. It's a pattern. My MO. Whatever the fuck you want to call it."

"Okay. So why change the color of the trinkets? Or right and left hands."

Kara shrugged. "I have to do things in sixes. I'm sure some shrink will have a field day with that one, but that's the only reason. I've always been surprised that the cops in Vermont never really picked up on the pillow thing. They just thought I was staging the scene. I'm a little surprised you didn't find those cases in your nationwide hunt these past couple of weeks."

"We're still looking," she said honestly. "Any

other murders you want to confess to, besides mine?"

"And Jag's and Tina's?"

Callie sucked in a deep breath. "Are they dead?"

"Not yet." She curled her fingers around Callie's forearm. "Let's go join them."

"How about I join you?" Jag's voice jumped through the air, landing on her eardrums with a solid beat.

Kara pressed the cold metal of the gun into her temple and stood behind Callie. "What the fuck?" Kara asked with an angry grunt. "Where's Tina?"

Jag raised his palms to the sky and inched forward. "Not here."

"Don't come any closer, or I'll kill her," Kara said.

Jag stopped moving.

Callie tried to heave in a breath, but she couldn't. Panic settled into her chest. Her heart beat so irrationally she wondered if it might stop altogether. She stared into Jag's dark gaze, looking for some kind of solution.

His eyes shifted to the right and then back to her. He did that three times.

The third time she followed where his eyes took

her, and it landed her gaze right on the weapon in Kara's hand.

"Why don't you point that thing at me, because you don't want to hurt her. You need Callie," Jag said. He lowered his chin slightly, as if to tell Callie to trust him and go along.

She swallowed and gave him a slight nod. She'd be ready. She only hoped she'd understand the signal and that she wouldn't get him killed in the process.

Kara laughed. "Why?"

"To tell your story," Jag said. "You kill her, and the story changes focus. It won't be about you anymore. It will be about Callie, the reporter turned crime novelist who tried to take down the Trinket Killer but got her and her boyfriend killed instead. What a tragedy. Hell, I can even see a made for television movie out of this. But you won't be the heart of the story. You won't even have a point of view. In the fictionalized book version, you won't even be on the page."

Kara's grip tightened around Callie's arm so much that Callie thought it might cut off the circulation. Kara shifted her aim, pointing the gun at Jag. "I can't keep her alive now, and you know it."

"You've got a better chance of getting away

with killing me by keeping her alive and taking her hostage."

Kara tossed her head back and laughed.

Jag mouthed, *now*, and nodded.

Callie held her breath and lunged to the side, hitting Kara as hard as she could with her shoulder, knocking her off-balance.

Bang!

Callie fell on top of Kara as the gun flew to the ground, landing about five feet away.

Thud.

"Fuck," Jag said with a groan as he held his hand over the right part of his chest.

Kara kicked Callie off her and crawled toward the weapon.

Callie did her best to try to stop her but with her hands tied it was nearly impossible.

Jag jumped to his feet, holding his hand over a bloody wound as he raced toward them, but skidded to a stop as Kara lay on the muddy ground with the gun once again pointed at Jag.

"You stupid fucking asshole," Kara said as she rose.

"I'm not as stupid as you think." Jag dropped to his knees. Blood trickled down his arm.

"Put down the weapon," a woman's voice called. "Or I'll shoot."

Callie rolled to her side and let out a sigh of relief as she stared at Jenna and three other police officers, all pointing their weapons at Kara.

"You kill me. They kill you. It's just a lot of fucking paperwork," Jag said with a raspy breath. He fell to his back. "I hope someone called an ambulance, because I think I need one."

Callie tried to scramble to her feet, but she couldn't.

Footsteps stomped past her. One officer took the gun from Kara, slamming her up against the car.

"Hang on," Jenna whispered. "Let me cut the tape."

"Jag." Callie had to get to him. Tears burned her cheeks as they poured down her face. All she could see was him lying flat on his back, his legs stretched out. One of the cops knelt next to him. She couldn't even tell if he was still breathing. "How did you know we were here?"

"When we're on duty, we use Find My iPhone. Kara had his this whole time. And then Tina called 9-1-1 and confirmed the location. I'm just sorry we didn't get here before the bitch shot him."

Sirens rang out just as Jenna freed Callie's hands. "Thank you." She raced to Jag's side.

His face was drained of all color. His eyes were closed, and his breath was shallow.

She glanced at the other police officer who was placing pressure on his wound. He had a grim expression. "You fight, Jagar Bowie. You hear me. I promised you three months. But I really want a lifetime. I love you, so you better not die on me, asshole; you got that?"

"What she said," the officer said.

Callie sat in the corner of the waiting room. Jag's wound had required a dangerous surgery to remove the bullet from one of his heart chambers. Without the surgery, he'd surely die.

But the procedure itself could kill him as well.

The doors swished open; however, it was a doctor for another family.

She let out a long breath and went back to sipping the shitty hospital coffee.

"How are you holding up?" Henrietta, his mother, asked as she took the seat next to her, offering her a muffin.

"I'm okay." She shook her head. "No, thank you. I'm not hungry."

"It's been almost twenty-four hours, and you haven't eaten anything. You need to eat, dear." Henrietta shoved it in her hand.

Callie took it and gave her a weak smile. She glanced up and looked around the room. Ziggy and Jag's father stood by the vending machines while Darcie lay sprawled out on one of the hard benches with her head in Troy's lap. Part of Callie wanted to run. She didn't belong with his family. If it wasn't for her bringing Kara back, Jag wouldn't be fighting for his life right now.

"Thank you," Callie managed to choke out.

"He's going to pull through." Henrietta patted her leg. "He's a Bowie, and we're fighters."

"That he is." Callie nodded. "I'm sorry," she whispered.

"For what?"

Callie set both her coffee and muffin on the table and cupped her face. She couldn't stop the floodgates if she tried. At least they were silent tears, and no one had to hear them. Only her shoulders bobbed up and down like a crazy person.

"Oh, honey, if you're thinking this is your fault,

you better stop that now." Henrietta wrapped an arm around Callie and stroked her hair.

"It is my fault." Callie sucked in a breath and stiffened her spine. "Besides me bringing all this back to Seattle, he all but begged her to shoot him instead of me."

"That's kind of what cops do," Henrietta said. "And he loves you."

Callie turned her head and stared into the sweetest, kindest, most loving eyes. They were filled with understanding and forgiveness. Warmth and gratitude. Callie opened her mouth, but no words came out. She cleared her throat and tried again. "So many people died because of me and that book and now Jag—"

"You better not talk like that in front of my son," Harold said, standing over her with his hands on his hips. "The only person to blame in all of this is Kara or Carol or whatever the fuck that woman's name is. Frankly, this family is damn happy to have you back. Our son was miserable without you. Now once this surgery is over and he wakes up, I hope you won't be talking like that. And please tell me you're staying."

"As long as Jag wants me to, yes," she said.

"Good." Harold sat down on the other side of

her and took her hand and kissed the back of it. "Did you know we made it to the hospital just as the helicopter landed with Jag on it?"

She shook her head.

"We got to see him right before they wheeled him into the OR," Harold said. "He asked me to do him a favor."

"What's that?"

"He wanted you to know that he heard you. Loud and clear."

She smiled.

The doors into the waiting room opened and in walked the surgeon. Everyone stood and inched toward the doctor. It was eerily quiet.

Callie stayed one step back, but that changed when Henrietta and Harold pulled her front and center.

"How is he?" Troy broke the silence.

"The surgery went very well. Better than anticipated. The bullet didn't do nearly as much damage as we thought. He'll make a full recovery, though it will take some time."

"When can we see him?" Henrietta asked.

Callie clutched her chest. The words *full recovery* echoed in her brain.

"He's actually awake and giving all of us a hard

time, even though he's groggy. But he's in the recovery room, so I can only let in two at a time, for short periods, and only immediate family for the next twenty-four hours. While we don't see any problems or complications arising, we have to be cautious," the doctor said.

Immediate family. Well, he was alive. That's all that mattered.

"Excuse me, Doctor, but is a fiancée considered immediate family?" Henrietta asked.

"Of course," the doctor said.

Callie's jaw slacked open. She might have been that once, but she wasn't his fiancée now.

Henrietta turned and dug into her purse. "My husband wasn't totally honest about his conversation with our son before they took him into the OR."

"I'm not following," Callie said.

"He was lucid enough to ask us to get this from his house." She pulled out the jewelry box that housed her engagement ring. "I think he wanted us to go in first so he could give it to you, but this is the only way to get you to him." She took the ring out and slipped it on Callie's finger. "Why don't you go see him first? Alone."

"I... I..." Callie blinked, staring at the shiny diamond.

"Just go tell my son you love him." Henrietta kissed her cheek. "We're all so happy you came home."

Every single time Jag shifted, his entire chest felt like he ripped it open. But he couldn't get comfortable.

"You can have more pain meds," the nurse said as she fiddled with the IV drip.

"No. I'm groggy enough," he said. "I want to be alert so I can talk with my family. Aren't they coming?"

"The doctor went to go get them." She rested the call button on the side of his bed. "Use this if you need me and use this one"—she held up another wire with a button on the end of it—"when you want pain meds. If I were you, I'd give yourself a few pumps now. I'll make sure we weaken the dosage for you. Just do one or two now. Trust me, you won't be sleeping from it, and you might be able to get comfortable."

He took it and tapped it once. "Thanks."

An immediate tingle filtered through his bloodstream. She was right; it didn't make him groggy, but he wasn't going to risk a second shot. Not until after he got to see Callie.

The nurse pulled back the fabric, and his breath hitched.

"Hey," Callie whispered.

"Hey, yourself." His pulse increased, and it showed on the monitor as it beeped a little faster. "You look like shit."

She chuckled. "You look a hell of a lot better than the last time I saw you." She inched closer.

He patted the side of the gurney.

"I don't want to hurt you."

"It will hurt me if I don't at least get to hold your hand."

She smiled, easing herself to the side of the bed, barely resting her ass against the mattress. "I hope I did the right thing."

"What are you talking about?"

"I thought you wanted me to tackle her, but now I'm not so sure."

He chuckled, but it was cut short by the pain. He clutched his chest. "You did exactly what I wanted. I just didn't expect the gun to discharge, and I thought Jenna was closer."

"You knew she was there?"

"I could see the patrol car through the trees behind you. Kara couldn't see it. My calculations were a little off though." He took in a slow breath, trying not to breathe too deep because it fucking hurt. He took her hand and gasped. "Have I been asleep for three months?" He ran his finger over the diamond shining bright on her hand.

"Oh. Well, that's the only way the hospital would let me in to see you. Immediate family only."

The corners of his mouth tugged into a smile. "But you put it on, and you told me you wanted more than three months. You said you wanted a lifetime." He lifted her hand and kissed her ring finger. "When I saw Kara holding that gun to your head, I thought my heart stopped."

"It almost did," she said.

He arched a brow. "That's really not funny."

"I know. Sorry, but you know how I get when you get all mushy and shit."

"I love you, Callie. I never stopped, and I want you in my life always. I'm not asking for you to say yes right now, but I am asking—"

"Yes," she said, tears rolling down her cheeks. "I want to marry you."

"You do?" He tilted his head. "You're not going to make me grovel and beg?"

She leaned over and pressed her warm lips against his. "No. But I do have a condition."

"Oh shit. Here it comes," he said, lifting the pain med controls. "Do I need to fill myself full of drugs for this?"

"You might," she said. "A while back you mentioned writing the book with me. Did you mean it?"

"Oh, that." He groaned as he lifted his hand and cupped her cheek, pulling her closer, feeling her hot breath on his skin. "Can I be the chief of police and co-write your book?"

"Yes," she whispered.

"Then you'll marry me?" he asked as if they both needed it to be official.

"Yes." She kissed him tenderly, resting her hand on his chest.

He moaned and not in a good way.

"Fuck, sorry." She bolted to a sitting position.

"No worries. It was worth it," he said, trying not to laugh because that would just make it worse.

"I should go so the rest of your family can come visit." She kissed his forehead and headed toward the curtain.

"Callie?"

She paused and glanced over her shoulder. "Yes?"

He smiled, letting out a long breath. "I love you."

"I love you right back."

EPILOGUE

THREE MONTHS LATER...

Jag rolled his wedding ring. How the world had changed in such a short period of time. He leaned against the railing of the front porch and blew into his coffee. He'd been married for less than twenty-four hours, and he was about to embark on a honeymoon to Hawaii.

He'd always wanted to go there but just never bothered. Not even to visit his brother, who came home often enough.

Of course, Jag just didn't take time off work unless forced. But the one time that happened, he wallowed in self-pity. A trip to Hawaii wouldn't have allowed him to do that.

The front door rattled and out walked his beautiful bride.

"Good morning, sunshine," he said, raising his mug. "Are you all packed?"

"I am." She leaned into him and gave him a long, wet, passionate kiss that by any standards would be considered a gross public display of affection.

He squeezed her ass. "We have time."

"Oh, no, we don't," she said with a laugh. "And we have plenty of time for wild sex all week."

"Yes, dear."

"You love saying that."

"Yes, dear. I do." He winked. If anyone told him he could be this happy, he'd wonder what that person was smoking. He had no idea life could be so fucking amazing.

She took his coffee cup and raised it to her lips. "I have some news I want to tell you before we head off this morning."

"And what's that?"

"You might want to sit down for this," she said.

He arched a brow. "This doesn't sound like a good way to start off a honeymoon."

"It depends on how you look at it."

"I'm not following," he said.

"Well. The good news is we don't have to pack

birth control, but the bad news is, it wasn't the chicken that made me sick the other day."

"Then what made you sick... oh." He scratched the side of his face as the first part of her sentence repeated in his mind. They hadn't really talked too much about having a family. Well, they did. In the future. Maybe in a year or two. "You're right. I need to sit down." He made himself comfortable on the love seat. "A baby?"

She handed him a white stick with a little window. Inside the window was the word *pregnant*. "I need to confirm with the doctor, and I don't want to tell anyone yet. Not until we get past the three-month mark because of what happened the last time."

"I understand," he said. "So, how long have you thought you might be?"

"I'm three weeks late."

"Three weeks?" He blinked, staring up at her. "Why didn't you tell me?"

"And freak you out before the wedding? No fucking way."

He pulled her to his lap. "I would have been fine. I think."

She laughed. "Are you okay with this?"

He smiled, resting his hand on her stomach.

Their child grew inside her belly. Just the thought squeezed at his heart. His chest tightened. "If it's a boy, can we name him David?"

"David Bowie? No fucking way. Not going to happen."

"My father tried to get my mom to do that for years," he said with a chuckle. "But in all seriousness, I do have a couple of names picked out."

"Really? You've known you were going to be a father for three and a half minutes, and you've got names."

"I've actually been thinking about them for a while now." He tilted her chin with his thumb and forefinger. "I thought if we had a boy, we could name him Steven, and if we had a girl—"

"Stephanie," she whispered.

He nodded.

"You really need to stop making me cry." She swiped at her face. "I love you, Jagar Harold Bowie."

"I love you right back, Callie Dixon Bowie."

Thank you for taking the time to read *Investigate Away*. I hope you enjoyed. Please feel free to leave an honest review.

The next book in this series is: *Sail Away*.

Sign up for my Newsletter (https://dl.bookfunnel.com/82gm8b9k4y) where I often give away free books before publication.

Join my private Facebook group (https://www.facebook.com/groups/191706547909047/) where I post exclusive excerpts and discuss all things murder and love!

ABOUT THE AUTHOR

Jen Talty is the *USA Today* Bestselling Author of Contemporary Romance, Romantic Suspense, and Paranormal Romance. In the fall of 2020, her short story was selected and featured in a 1001 Dark Nights Anthology.

Regardless of the genre, her goal is to take you on a ride that will leave you floating under the sun with warmth in your heart. She writes stories about broken heroes and heroines who aren't necessarily looking for romance, but in the end, they find the kind of love books are written about :).

She first started writing while carting her kids to one hockey rink after the other, averaging 170 games per year between 3 kids in 2 countries and 5 states. Her first book, IN TWO WEEKS was originally published in 2007. In 2010 she helped form a publishing company (Cool Gus Publishing) with *NY*

Times Bestselling Author Bob Mayer where she ran the technical side of the business through 2016.

Jen is currently enjoying the next phase of her life…the empty nester! She and her husband reside in Jupiter, Florida.

Grab a glass of vino, kick back, relax, and let the romance roll in…

Sign up for my Newsletter (https://dl.bookfunnel.com/82gm8b9k4y) where I often give away free books before publication.

Join my private Facebook group (https://www.facebook.com/groups/191706547909047/) where I post exclusive excerpts and discuss all things murder and love!

Never miss a new release. Follow me on Amazon: amazon.com/author/jentalty

And on Bookbub: bookbub.com/authors/jen-talty

ALSO BY JEN TALTY

Brand new series: SAFE HARBOR!

MINE TO KEEP

MINE TO SAVE

MINE TO PROTECT

Check out LOVE IN THE ADIRONDACKS!

SHATTERED DREAMS

AN INCONVENIENT FLAME

THE WEDDING DRIVER

NY STATE TROOPER SERIES (also set in the Adirondacks!)

In Two Weeks

Dark Water

Deadly Secrets

Murder in Paradise Bay

To Protect His own

Deadly Seduction

When A Stranger Calls

His Deadly Past

The Corkscrew Killer

Brand New Novella for the First Responders series

A spin-off from the NY State Troopers series

PLAYING WITH FIRE

PRIVATE CONVERSATION

THE RIGHT GROOM

AFTER THE FIRE

CAUGHT IN THE FLAMES

CHASING THE FIRE

Legacy Series

Dark Legacy

Legacy of Lies

Secret Legacy

Colorado Brotherhood Protectors

Fighting For Esme

Defending Raven

Fay's Six

Yellowstone Brotherhood Protectors

Guarding Payton

Candlewood Falls
RIVERS EDGE
THE BURIED SECRET
ITS IN HIS KISS
LIPS OF AN ANGEL

It's all in the Whiskey
JOHNNIE WALKER
GEORGIA MOON
JACK DANIELS
JIM BEAM
WHISKEY SOUR
WHISKEY COBBLER
WHISKEY SMASH
IRISH WHISKEY

The Monroes
COLOR ME YOURS
COLOR ME SMART
COLOR ME FREE
COLOR ME LUCKY

COLOR ME ICE
COLOR ME HOME

Search and Rescue
PROTECTING AINSLEY
PROTECTING CLOVER
PROTECTING OLYMPIA
PROTECTING FREEDOM
PROTECTING PRINCESS
PROTECTING MARLOWE

DELTA FORCE-NEXT GENERATION
SHIELDING JOLENE
SHIELDING AALYIAH
SHIELDING LAINE
SHIELDING TALULLAH
SHIELDING MARIBEL

The Men of Thief Lake
REKINDLED
DESTINY'S DREAM

Federal Investigators

JANE DOE'S RETURN

THE BUTTERFLY MURDERS

THE AEGIS NETWORK

The Sarich Brother

THE LIGHTHOUSE

HER LAST HOPE

THE LAST FLIGHT

THE RETURN HOME

THE MATRIARCH

More Aegis Network

MAX & MILIAN

A CHRISTMAS MIRACLE

SPINNING WHEELS

HOLIDAY'S VACATION

Special Forces Operation Alpha

BURNING DESIRE

BURNING KISS

BURNING SKIES

BURNING LIES

BURNING HEART

BURNING BED

REMEMBER ME ALWAYS

The Brotherhood Protectors

Out of the Wild

ROUGH JUSTICE

ROUGH AROUND THE EDGES

ROUGH RIDE

ROUGH EDGE

ROUGH BEAUTY

The Brotherhood Protectors

The Saving Series

SAVING LOVE

SAVING MAGNOLIA

SAVING LEATHER

Hot Hunks

Cove's Blind Date Blows Up

My Everyday Hero – Ledger

Tempting Tavor

Malachi's Mystic Assignment

Needing Neor

Holiday Romances

A CHRISTMAS GETAWAY

ALASKAN CHRISTMAS WHISPERS

CHRISTMAS IN THE SAND

Heroes & Heroines on the Field

TAKING A RISK

TEE TIME

A New Dawn

THE BLIND DATE

SPRING FLING

SUMMERS GONE

WINTER WEDDING

THE AWAKENING

The Collective Order

THE LOST SISTER

THE LOST SOLDIER

THE LOST SOUL

THE LOST CONNECTION

THE NEW ORDER

www.ingramcontent.com/pod-product-compliance
Lightning Source LLC
Chambersburg PA
CBHW052145100425
24953CB00010B/361